"Here's to Ginny Selton, quitter and coward," Noah said.

"You can't admit you were wrong, can you? You can't admit you quit the hospital because of your desire for me."

"You're incredible, Grady!" Gin snapped. "Now you've decided that I'm not only incompetent, but I'm also some sex-starved idiot just dying to make love to you. Well, I don't intend to listen to your demented ravings."

"It's about time someone showed you you're just as fallible as the rest of us humans," Noah retorted, his body becoming taut with anger. "I should just shake some sense into that thick, stubborn skull of yours."

Before she realized what he was doing, he pulled her toward him, pressing her against the hard length of his body and kissing her, his lips harsh and demanding.

She struggled desperately, fighting not only Noah but also the sudden onrush of fire he was stirring in her treacherous body. She tried to deny the overwhelming urge to kiss him back, but desire spread like molten fire through her body. Her heart roared and pounded in her ears, obliterating all other sounds.

"I want you, Ginny," he whispered into her ear, his breath tantalizing her. "And I know you want me."

Dear Reader:

After more than one year of publication, SECOND CHANCE AT LOVE has a lot to celebrate. Not only has it become firmly established as a major line of paperback romances, but response from our readers also continues to be warm and enthusiastic. Your letters keep pouring in—and we love receiving them. We're getting to know you—your likes and dislikes—and want to assure you that your contribution does make a difference.

As we work hard to offer you better and better SECOND CHANCE AT LOVE romances, we're especially gratified to hear that you, the reader, are rating us higher and higher. After all, our success depends on *you*. We're pleased that you enjoy our books and that you appreciate the extra effort our writers and staff put into them. Thanks for spreading the good word about SECOND CHANCE AT LOVE and for giving us your loyal support. Please keep your suggestions and comments coming!

With warm wishes,

Ellen Edwards

Ellen Edwards
SECOND CHANCE AT LOVE
The Berkley/Jove Publishing Group
200 Madison Avenue
New York, NY 10016

Second Chance at Love

A FLAME TOO FIERCE
JAN MATHEWS

SECOND CHANCE AT LOVE
BOOK

A FLAME TOO FIERCE

Requests for permission to make copies of any part of the work should be
mailed to: Permissions, Second Chance at Love, The Berkley/Jove Publishing Group, 200 Madison Avenue, New York, NY 10016

First edition published September 1982

First printing

"Second Chance at Love" and the butterfly emblem are trademarks be-
longing to Jove Publications, Inc.

Printed in the United States of America

Second Chance at Love books are published by
The Berkley/Jove Publishing Group
200 Madison Avenue, New York, NY 10016

To garage sales, with gratitude—
and to my husband and children,
with more gratitude.

chapter 1

GIN SELTON sighed with relief and pushed a strand of long blond hair out of her eyes and into the twist at the back of her head. Visiting hours were finally over. She was exhausted, but there was still so much to do that she knew she'd never get off duty on time. So much for a two-week orientation, she thought, heading down the empty hallway. Today was only her second day on duty in this hospital and already two nurses had called in sick. The evening supervisor had made it clear that no other nurses were available to help. It was unfortunate, but Gin would have to manage more than her share of patients.

She checked the time as she entered a room. "Hi, Mr. Murphy," she said to the man lying on the bed, his flaccid arm propped up on a pillow. She felt for his pulse, then looked critically at the line of stitches on his shaved head.

"H-hi, G-G-Gin," the man answered over the din of the television. His words were thick and slightly slurred.

Gin glanced up at the screen. "Minnesota and Tampa Bay?" she asked.

The man started to stutter again, then grew red in the face. "It's Minnesota by a field goal," he said with a scowl when the words finally formed.

"It'll get better, Mr. Murphy." Gin smiled in sympathy.

"The little synapses in your brain that control your speech patterns will connect again when the swelling goes down. A few more days in therapy and you'll be *announcing* the game."

Looking reassured, Mr. Murphy nodded. "R-running late?" he asked as she glanced again at her watch.

"Always, Mr. Murphy. We're chronically understaffed here at the beautiful downtown Hilton. Now, let's see how well-oriented you are. Name?" She lifted her eyebrows inquiringly.

Mr. Murphy started to stutter again, but he was smiling. "K-K-Kojak." He laughed.

Gin giggled back at him when he grabbed a lollipop from his bedside table and popped it into his mouth. "My g-grandson," he finally said, indicating the candy.

"Well, I guess that's oriented enough." Gin laughed again as she checked his pupil response, then held her hands out for him to squeeze. "But you know, orders are orders, Mr. Murphy."

"Ch-check me every hour or the senior resident will gobble you up, huh?" Mr. Murphy twisted his lips into a snarl and tried to growl.

"I remind you, Mr. Murphy, Little Red Riding Hood won that battle." Noticing the sudden frown on his face, Gin touched his hand. "Something wrong?" she asked.

"I-I s-start radiation tomorrow," he said. He looked worried. "What do you think, Gin?"

"About radiation?" Gin was anxious to leave the room—it was getting so late—but she couldn't ignore the plea in Mr. Murphy's eyes.

"Is it worth it?" he asked. "Why go through the sickness and pain?"

"Have you talked with the doctors about the alternatives?" Gin sat down on the edge of a chair, trying to appear calm and unhurried.

"Oh s-sure. Th-they rush in and out of here, tell me what to do and how to feel, and not one of them, including the mighty Dr. Grady, has the guts to tell me what the heck a glioblastoma does."

"Mr. Murphy." Gin took a deep breath, reminded once again of the fine line between doctors and patients that nurses were expected to walk. "It's *your* body. Insist on some answers." She stood up to leave, knowing she had also cheated him. "Tell you what," she added. "I'll leave a note on the front of your chart for Dr. Grady. He can't give you radiation tomorrow without your consent. *Make* him give you an explanation." She left the room, calling over her shoulder, "I'll be back later to see what team won."

Gin sailed down the hall. She'd really have to hurry now. Medications were due. Mentally listing all the tasks she had to finish before the end of her shift, she shook the small pocket flashlight she used to check the dilation of her patients' pupils. Great time for the darned batteries to go dead, she fumed, rounding the corner sharply—and gasping as she collided with a man's tall, muscular form.

"Oh, excuse me!" Gin watched helplessly as the charts in the man's hands spilled all over the floor.

"I see we have another highly capable, efficient nurse on this unit," he grumbled, sarcastically, glaring down at the mess of papers littering the shiny tile.

Gin bent to pick up the charts, trying to reorganize

them quickly. "You must be Dr. Michaels, the resident on call," she said. "I'm Gin Selton, and I apologize for my clumsiness."

"Suspicions confirmed!" He grabbed the charts from her as she stood up to face him. Suddenly she was overwhelmed by a sense of powerful masculinity. "You're not even intelligent enough to read name tags. I'm Dr. Grady, senior resident, Neurosurgery," he told her, then narrowed his silver-gray eyes and glared at her. "Nurses at Lakeside General learn quickly, especially if they value their jobs."

"I apologize profusely, *Dr. Grady*. Both for knocking the charts from your hands and for not recognizing you." Unaccountably breathless, Gin glared back at the devastatingly handsome man standing before her. He must be in his mid-thirties, she thought, but his rugged physique and thick black hair suggested a younger man. To her dismay, Gin's pulse raced at the mere sight of him. Finally she gathered her thoughts together enough to connect the names and said, "I hope you're seeing Mr. Murphy tonight. He has several unanswered questions." She couldn't stop a note of sarcasm from creeping into her voice.

"Which I'm sure you took it upon yourself to answer—incorrectly, no doubt." Grady slammed closed a file and scowled down at her, then stalked off, his white lab coat billowing out behind him.

Gin glared after him, then headed for the nurses' station. What a detestable man! She should have known better than to come to another major medical center. They were all alike—filled with pathetic, seriously ill patients and egotistical doctors who expected their nurses to perform miracles. No wonder there was so much staff turnover. Gin sighed in frustration as she entered the medication room.

"Did you see Dr. Grady?" Suzanne Bonati, the

other nurse on duty, inquired. "He was looking for you."

"Grady? Don't you mean Hitler?" Gin answered as she flipped through her medication cards. "Oh, yes. We ran into each other in the hall."

Suzanne laughed. "That's a great nickname for him. Although I doubt if even Adolf Hitler was as conceited as Grady. The man is on a real ego trip."

"So I just learned." Gin turned away and started to set up her medications.

"Well, I guess the fantastic Noah Grady does have a right to be just a bit vain," Suzanne said. "He's a great neurosurgeon, and did you notice that body of his? He's built like a Greek god. I swear he's Adonis reincarnated, only with dark hair and gray eyes." She giggled, then continued. "And on the hospital sex scale he rates a nine point eight. Every nurse who works here would give her eyeteeth for one night with him!"

"Is his rating accurate?" Gin asked, annoyed to feel her pulse racing again.

"A girl can dream." Suzanne laughed. "Maybe we can get stranded here by one of the Minnesota blizzards and find out. Oh, don't mind me, Gin. Since I've been pregnant, I've been terribly sensual."

"It's the hormones," Gin explained. She mixed a vial of antibiotics and drew the liquid into a syringe.

"I don't know what it is, but if I keep it up, my husband's going to keel over with heart failure." Suzanne looked out the door, then lowered her voice to a whisper. "Look out! Hitler's back!"

"Where the hell is that new nurse?" Grady demanded of Suzanne.

Gin groaned at the sound of his voice, but walked calmly into the nurses' station to face him. "What do you need, Dr. Grady?"

"Nothing's been charted on these patients! How am I to assess their condition when the nurses take it upon themselves to ignore my orders?" Grady threw the charts on the desk.

"I haven't had time to chart yet, Dr. Grady." It was all Gin could do to respond civilly to him. "I've carried out your orders explicitly, Doctor, except that I haven't taken Mr. DeRocco's vitals every two hours. I've been too busy. All the information is here on my board, if you'd care to look."

"I don't suppose anyone told you that when I make my rounds I expect everything to be on the patient's chart. And as far as Mr. DeRocco's vital signs are concerned, if you can't manage to take them as ordered, then this unit isn't for you. Maybe you should ask for a transfer."

"Dr. Grady." Gin clenched her fists at her sides. This was the wrong way to start out with any doctor. "Neuro is my specialty. I did assess Mr. DeRocco, and he was stable. I decided some of the other patients needed my expertise more."

"When Mr. DeRocco was admitted, Miss Selton," Dr. Grady began in an even tone, his gray eyes snapping and his body taut with unleashed tension, "he was in a state of status epilepticus. He had to be placed on a respirator. I've managed to control him for two weeks now, but he's still a keg of dynamite. Now, what authorized you to ignore my specific orders?"

"Nursing judgment," Gin responded angrily. "Perhaps some of your orders are unnecessary." As soon as the words were out of her mouth, Gin regretted them. She shouldn't have questioned his authority, even if she did think she was right.

"Is it also 'nursing judgment' to tell a patient he has a right to *refuse* radiation?" Grady said in a low voice of such angry intensity that Gin took an involuntary step backward.

"I told Mr. Murphy to ask you about alternatives, Dr. Grady. He has a right to know!" Gin's voice was equally intense, and she trembled with anger.

Grady pointed a finger at his broad chest. "*I* alone determine what and when a patient is to be told something!" He slammed Mr. Murphy's chart into the rack and whirled back to face her. "Don't forget that, Miss Selton!"

Gin resisted the impulse to slap the smug look off his face and instead threw her board on the desk. She turned and stalked back to the medication room.

She met Suzanne's wide, sympathetic eyes as she walked in. "Jeez, Gin, don't you value your license?" Suzanne said. "Grady's God around here."

"I don't care who he is," Gin retorted. "No doctor is going to get away with treating me so rudely." She finished preparing the medications and hurried down the hall.

Several hours after Grady had left the unit in a state of upheaval, Gin was still upset over her encounter with him. She sighed at the stack of charts on her desk, which had begun to resemble an impenetrable mountain, and scrawled her name across a page of orders. She had certainly had a long and frustrating night, she thought as she glanced up at the clock. Even that seemed to be conspiring against her—it was almost eleven P.M.!

Gin walked wearily down the hall. "I'm going to check on Mr. DeRocco again, Suzanne," she called back over her shoulder.

"Anything I can help you with?" Suzanne offered. "I think you got the heavy hall tonight."

"No. I just want to check in on him. The last time I was in the room he was acting a little suspicious. But it's probably just my overworked imagination, especially after what Dr. Grady put me through earlier."

Gin entered Mr. DeRocco's room, her thoughts on her aching feet. She flipped on a small side light. There was no need to wake her patient if he was resting comfortably, she reasoned, then froze. Mr. DeRocco was in the middle of a seizure! His lips were turning blue, and he was gasping for breath.

"Oh my God!" Gin groaned, pressing the emergency button on the wall.

"Get Dr. Michaels!" she shouted into the intercom. "And bring the emergency cart!"

Suzanne arrived moments later with the supplies, and Gin quickly inserted a needle into Mr. DeRocco's vein, then hung the intravenous fluid. "Get that airway in!" she ordered. When Suzanne hesitated, she barked, "Are you with me or not, Suzanne?"

Her eyes wide with fear, the other nurse finally sprang into action. "God, Gin," she said, her voice trembling, "they can't find Dr. Michaels. He doesn't answer his page."

Gin glanced at Mr. DeRocco, whose body continued to jerk, then back at Suzanne. "How about Dr. Grady? Is he still around?"

"Grady'll have a fit when he sees this." Suzanne ran to the hall telephone, then returned shortly. "He's coming," she said. "Gin, he was furious. I think he's going to have your hide."

Ignoring Suzanne's remark, Gin worked desperately to revive Mr. DeRocco. She could hear the page still calling Dr. Grady to the room. "How long do elevators take around here?" she wailed, the helplessness of her situation infuriating her. Her education had more than adequately prepared her for this kind of crisis, but she couldn't do anything else without a physician's direct order.

Relief seeped through her when she finally heard the approach of the emergency team hurrying down the hall. Within moments an assemblage of personnel and equipment barreled into the room, followed a few seconds later by Dr. Grady, who glared at her, clenching his jaw, then began to issue orders in a rapid-fire voice.

Each passing minute seemed like hours to Gin. She automatically followed his sharp commands while they worked desperately together to resuscitate the patient. She had almost forgotten their previous encounter, but when Mr. DeRocco finally began to stabilize, Grady's cool, collected manner changed into an expression of fury, and he glowered at Gin over the bed.

She cringed inwardly as she met his riveting silver gaze. His earlier anger was nothing compared to the look on his face now.

"So much for your 'nursing judgment,' Miss Selton." Grady's caustic voice drew the immediate attention of everyone in the room. "I'll leave further orders at the desk. Make sure they're carried out this time."

"Dr. Grady . . ." Suzanne held up an empty bottle of bourbon before Gin could form a reply. "I just found this in Mr. DeRocco's bedside table while I was looking for some tape."

Grady reached for the bottle and swore under his breath. "I've told him over and over what alcohol could do to his disease!" he snapped, then, throwing the empty bottle in a nearby trash can, he turned back to Gin. "However, that still doesn't excuse *your* neglect, Miss Selton. Now, if you'll please take the patient's blood pressure and check his pupils every fifteen minutes—or aren't you competent enough to do that?"

As members of the emergency team fell into shocked silence, Gin struggled to preserve a few shreds of professional dignity. How dare he blame her for this! His comments about her competence were excessively cruel. "Yes, Dr. Grady, I am fully capable of checking Mr. DeRocco's pulse and pupils. And for your information, I had you paged because Dr. Michaels didn't answer his page." She held her voice in check, though she was seething with anger.

"*Dr.* Michaels is in the operating room, Miss Selton, performing surgery on a patient from Intensive Care." Grady looked even more furious.

"If you knew that, Dr. Grady, then you should have assigned someone to cover!" Gin shot back as Grady stalked out of the room.

Determined to ignore his biting comments, Gin turned quickly back to her patient. She moved about the room, efficiently performing the many tasks that would help keep him alive, her calm demeanor belying the intensity of her anger.

It was almost dawn when Gin finished work and punched out. Her feet felt like lead weights, and she slipped them from her pinching shoes, enjoying the feel of the cold tiles on her hot toes. Her shoulders ached, and she could barely keep her eyes open.

She placed her head on the cool metal time clock for a moment, then inhaled deeply, shaking her head to clear it. Thank goodness the drive home wasn't long, she thought, then realized she'd forgotten to fill up the gas tank. She slipped her shoes back on, frustrated with her lack of forethought. Now, after working practically a double shift, she'd have to stop for gas.

Mumbling to herself, she turned to leave and stopped short when she almost collided with Noah Grady once again. He stood beside her looking well rested and refreshed—and even sexier than before. Gin stifled an immediate rush of anger and ignored the quickening of her pulse. Such an egotistical man had no right to look so good.

"Meet me at The Nook, Selton. We need to have a little talk," he ordered.

The Nook was the local hospital hangout, a greasy spoon frequented twenty-four hours a day by nurses, interns, and residents. Gin definitely didn't feel like going there now.

"I'm very tired, Dr. Grady. Mr. DeRocco is stable. Is it important?"

"Extremely so, Selton." Grady stalked out, not even waiting for her assent.

She should just go home, Gin fumed, but she knew a confrontation with Grady was imminent and unavoidable. A command was a command. She sighed. Starting off with Grady like this, she'd be lucky if she kept her job another week.

In the parking lot her car coughed and sputtered, but started at last. She scraped the thick layer of ice from the windows, still considering whether to ignore Grady's command and probably face her supervisor tomorrow.

She shivered getting back into the car and shifted the gears angrily. At the stoplight she turned left toward The Nook, driving faster than usual and pulling to an abrupt halt in the parking lot.

Inside the crowded room Gin glanced around until she found Grady in a corner booth. The restaurant was filled with hospital personnel, including several people she recognized from the emergency team she'd worked with earlier. She nodded at them as she wove her way toward Grady and sat down without a word. Tucking her coat snugly around her, she glared at him. Two cups of steaming coffee already stood on the table, the sight of which sent her anger soaring still higher. Obviously he hadn't even *considered* the possibility that she might not show up!

Grady glanced at her briefly and indicated the coffee. "I don't know what your educational qualifications are, Miss Selton," he began without preamble, "but I have serious doubts about how you're going to work out at Lakeside." His voice was clipped and cold, and he sipped the scalding coffee as if it were ice water, his expression as cool as his voice. "But I've decided to give you another chance. We've started out on the wrong foot, and I'm prepared to forget last night's incidents. But don't cross me again. Although we desperately need nurses in my unit, and I would hate to have you dismissed over something that might very well be a misunderstanding, I want to stress that from now on I will not tolerate your insolent attitude."

Gin seethed with silent fury throughout his speech, but managed to bite her tongue. It galled her to think she was sitting here so calmly, dead tired, listening to an egotistical doctor expound on her lack of qualifications.

Bitterly she wished she could walk away from his arrogant lecture but she certainly didn't want to lose her job. Having just moved across the country to Minneapolis, she wasn't ready to relocate again. Besides the time and finances involved in job searching, she didn't have the emotional stamina to leave Lakeside Hospital, especially now when she was trying so hard to get over the death of her parents.

As Grady continued to talk, she was reminded vividly of the other reason she'd moved to Minnesota. Noah Grady's personality was so much like Nick's it was painful. For a moment her former fiancé's handsome features flitted through her mind, but she shoved the memory aside. It wouldn't do any good to think about that part of her past. She tried to tell herself that what she felt for Nick was dead, but she realized the wounds were still fresh.

Gin sipped the bitter coffee and listened to Grady outline everything he expected from his nurses. When he was finished, she placed her cup on the table, willing her trembling hands to stop shaking.

She tossed her head back defiantly. Job or no job, she had tolerated enough of his insults. "Dr. Grady," she began in an even voice that vibrated with anger, "I graduated from the University of Virginia, cum laude, then took an extended course in neurology from Johns Hopkins. I worked for three years in the neuro intensive care unit at Duke University before I moved here." She paused for breath, then flipped two quarters on the table. "I don't know why you're trying to crucify me, Grady, but thanks for the coffee."

Gin walked quickly out of the restaurant, holding her head high and ignoring the knowing stares of medical personnel jammed into several of the booths. Noah Grady was grating on her nerves, and for some reason she felt he was purposely trying to persecute her.

chapter 2

"THOUGHT I'D warn you, Gin," Suzanne Bonati said under her breath. "Hitler just got out of the elevator."

"Good grief, Suzanne! Don't call him that here," Gin replied. "If it gets back to him I started that, he'll have my job for certain."

"Things have been going okay for the last few weeks, haven't they?" Suzanne giggled. "Besides, the name's all over the hospital. The operator almost called him that over the pager last night."

"Good evening, Miss Selton, Mrs. Bonati." Grady walked over to the charts, pulling out those marked with orange tags. "How's Mr. Murphy tonight?" he asked Gin.

"Sick from radiation," she said briskly, their verbal battle over the patient still fresh in her mind. "I just gave him a shot to make him feel better."

"Good. Let's keep him comfortable." Grady began to leaf through the charts.

"Dr. Grady." Gin took a deep breath. She dreaded

his reaction to her request and hated to create further animosity between them, but her patient was important to her. "Could you check in on Mrs. St. John before you leave? I'm a little concerned about her."

Grady looked up and raised an inquiring eyebrow at her. "What's her neurological status?"

"Stable. And so are her vitals. She's set up for an angiogram tomorrow, but she just doesn't look good."

"Terrific." Grady scowled at her. "Very scientific observation, Miss Selton. Do you have anything intelligent to add?"

"Dr. Grady—"

Grady's biting voice cut her off. "I wouldn't look very good either, Miss Selton, if someone told me I might have a time bomb in my head. Now this patient has been examined by every resident and intern on my neurological service. *They* feel she's stable enough to wait for a confirmed diagnosis."

"Gee, thanks for checking her, Grady!" Gin snapped, turning away to give her full attention to the chart in front of her. Why he enjoyed berating her was beyond her comprehension, but she was beginning to lose her temper again.

"Oh yes, Miss Selton," Grady went on. "I forgot to mention that you seem to have been working out better these past weeks. Until tonight, that is." He left the station before she could respond, his heels echoing down the tile hallway, but Gin noted with satisfaction he was headed toward Mrs. St. John's room.

Suzanne shook her head and clucked in sympathy. "I don't believe him, Gin. Why didn't you smash that chart in his face?"

"I need the job," Gin returned dryly, wondering herself why she tolerated all the frustrations of her position. Sometimes any profession seemed preferable to nursing. "Single girls have to support themselves," she mumbled.

"I guess I can relate to that," Suzanne replied. "We need the extra money now, although Robert hates me working evenings. Say! Why don't we apply for a position with a moving company?" Suzanne chuckled. "The hours are great, and so's the pay."

"At the rate we move beds around here, we'd certainly be well qualified," Gin agreed, laughing with her.

"Or how about engineering?" Suzanne suggested.

Gin shook her head. "Too many egotistical men. Speaking of which, who's on call tonight?"

Suzanne glanced at the schedule. "The infamous Dr. Michaels. Let's hope we don't have an emergency."

"Where does he always manage to hide?" Frowning, Gin replaced a chart in the rack.

"You got me. Grady keeps him on, too. I guess he thinks his residents are above reproach. Michaels usually has a believable excuse, though," she added.

Gin headed for the hall, pushing her medication cart in front of her. "Well, I'm worried about Mrs. St. John. Dr. Michaels had better be around if her aneurysm blows."

Suzanne frowned. "Gin! Don't say that!"

"Suzanne, I've got this horrid, irrational feeling of impending disaster. Great! Now I sound like a psychic! Look, forget I said anything." Gin pushed the cart around the corner.

Some time later she was scrawling her name on the last chart when Suzanne stood up to peer at the intercom. "That's Mrs. St. John's light." She glanced at Gin. "Do you want me to get it?"

"No," Gin rose from her chair. "I'll go. Aren't the

night nurses done listening to the tape recorded report yet?" she moaned as she left the station. "I'm beat."

"There's hope," Suzanne quipped. "We go off duty in two minutes."

Gin walked quickly toward her patient's room. The unexplained fears she'd had earlier in the evening rose in full force now. It was probably nothing, she tried to convince herself. The woman just needed a pill for the pain or some water. Lying quietly in a darkened room could grow wearisome, Gin told herself as she tried to push thoughts of disaster to the back of her mind. Mrs. St. John was a delightful person, constantly apologizing for her helplessness. She was always so pleased when Gin stole a few moments to sit and talk, and more than likely she just wanted some company now.

Gin called out her usual cheerful greeting when she entered the dark room, then automatically reached for the woman's pulse. It was racing. She flipped on a light. Mrs. St. John looked pale. Too pale.

"I'm sorry to bother you, Gin, but my head is killing me." The woman's speech was already slurred. "I didn't tell Dr. Grady earlier . . . I was . . . scared . . . but I can't . . . stand it . . . anymore." Her voice faded away.

Gin checked her pupils. They were sluggish and unequal, and her blood pressure had dropped drastically. She pressed the emergency button. "Call a code blue!" she screamed to Suzanne.

Minutes later the emergency team raced into the room. After they had stablized Mrs. St. John, an intern examined her. "There's almost nothing I can do for her," he said, finally shaking his head. He turned to Gin, his expression grim. "She's a bad risk, but there might be a chance if you call a neurosurgeon fast."

Gin glanced at the evening supervisor. "Where's

Dr. Michaels?" she asked, then scowled at her supervisor's shrug. "Well, why don't you look for him!" she snapped. "Try the linen closets."

Looking at her patient's pale face, Gin thought for a moment, then turned to Suzanne. "Stay with Mrs. St. John. I'm going to find Grady."

Ignoring the supervisor's negative command, she ran from the room. Her heart pounded and her hands shook as she dialed Grady's number.

"I'm sorry," the polite voice on the other end of the telephone said. "Dr. Grady isn't on call tonight. Try Dr. Michaels."

"I did." Gin exclaimed as she slammed down the receiver. She tapped her fingers on the desk, thinking about Mrs. St. John. The woman was going to die if she didn't do something!

"Who's with her?" Gin asked when Suzanne entered the station.

"Night nurses," her friend answered. "The supervisor's looking for Michaels. Did you get Grady?"

"What's Mary Anne Harner's number?"

"The Intensive Care nurse?" Suzanne stared incredulously at her.

"Yes. I overheard some recent gossip. Look up her number in the internal directory." Gin paged Dr. Michaels again while Suzanne flipped through the book.

"If Grady's there, you'll be hanging yourself," Suzanne said dryly, handing her the number. "Maybe the gossipmongers are wrong."

"Gossip's the one constant in this place," Gin snapped as she dialed the number. She prayed silently that she could find Grady before it was too late.

When Mary Anne Harner's sultry voice finally answered on the tenth ring, Gin was out of patience. "Get me Grady!" she snapped.

Mary Anne cleared her throat. "Pardon me?"

"This is Gin Selton from Neuro and I need Grady now!" Gin was furious with Michaels, with Grady, with herself—with the entire system.

"Look, Selton—" Mary Anne's voice was no longer sultry—"I've got a hot date in the bedroom, and he's one hell of a lover. Call Michaels if you need a neurosurgeon!"

"You listen to me!" Gin shouted, then lowered her voice. "Look, tell him to get his butt to the phone or I swear"—Gin clenched her teeth—"I'll come and drag him from your bed!"

The phone clunked in her ear, and within moments Grady's angry voice sounded from the other end. "Selton," he said, his voice icy, "just who the hell gave you this number?"

Gin's heart was pounding furiously. Thank God Grady was there! "Get your pants on, Dr. Grady. Mrs. St. John just blew her aneurysm, and I can't find Dr. Michaels."

"But you found me!" Grady snapped.

"Dr. Grady," Gin said, no longer able to contain her anger, "every animal has his habitat. Because of your stature in the hospital hierarchy, yours is just easier to find." She took a deep breath. "This is an emergency. Mrs. St. John is going to die!"

"Just like that," Grady exploded. "You're able to diagnose a ruptured aneurysm just like that! No X rays, no examination. Just intuition, I suppose."

"Grady, I don't have time to argue with you. Are you coming or not?"

Grady paused a moment, then sighed. "Yes, I'll be there in ten minutes."

"Oh, Dr. Grady." Gin hoped he hadn't already hung up. "I have the Decadron and Amicar ready. Shall I run them?"

"If you're wrong, Selton," Grady rasped, "and we administer Amicar, are you aware of what we could do to Mrs. St. John?"

"And if I'm right?" Gin answered, all business.

Another pause followed. From the way his voice had faded in and out, Gin suspected he'd been dressing as he talked.

"Run them," Grady finally said. "Call X Ray and have them set up for an emergency angiogram, and alert Surgery." His voice was clipped and professional. "And," he added, "keep her alive until I get there."

"Nobody dies on my shift, Grady," Gin whispered, then hung up the phone, grabbed the medications, and ran down the hall.

It was close to dawn when Gin caught the telephone at her bedside on the first ring. She had been too emotionally overwrought to sleep and was trying to read, hoping the novel would lull her into a stupor. She was surprised when she recognized Grady's voice.

"Mrs. St. John made it through surgery, Selton." He sounded weary. "She's in Intensive Care."

The tension drained from Gin's body. She genuinely liked Mrs. St. John. The woman's quiet voice and gentle ways reminded her of her own mother.

"She'll have some temporary paralysis on the left side, but with any luck at all she'll make it," Grady continued in a curt voice. "It was a berry aneurysm after all. We clipped it."

"I'm surprised you went in," Gin said.

"It was a calculated risk," Grady responded. "I just thought you'd like to know."

"Thanks, Grady," Gin answered, then replaced the receiver in its cradle. She padded to the bathroom, rebrushed her teeth, and fell into bed, exhaustion overwhelming her.

The sun was streaming into the room when she woke the following afternoon. She yawned and stretched lazily, then turned over, her eyes focusing on her clock. When the time actually penetrated fuzzy recesses of her brain, she jumped out of bed and ran into the bathroom. Damn! She was going to be late for work.

Half an hour later, Gin hurried from the parking lot. She hadn't realized the extent of her fatigue last night and still couldn't believe she'd slept through her alarm. She rushed into the building and, not bothering to wait for the elevators, ran up the three flights of stairs to the neurological unit.

"Sorry I'm late." She gave an apologetic smile to the other nurses who were gathered around the desk. "I overslept."

"Oh, Miss Selton," the ward clerk said, "the head nurse wants to see you in her office. I'll let her know you've finally arrived."

"Trouble?" Suzanne asked, a frown marring her forehead. "Do you think Grady reported you last night? You were awfully rough on him, you know."

Suzanne's comments reminded Gin of their frantic struggles to keep Mrs. St. John alive and of her fury at Grady when he finally arrived. She had to admit, though, that as much as Grady irritated her, she highly respected his medical skills.

"I don't think so, Suzanne," Gin reassured her co-worker. "I talked to Grady late last night, and he didn't seem upset. In fact, he was almost human. For once he didn't scream at me or act sarcastic. I just think our head nurse is about to deny my holiday request."

Suzanne grinned at Gin. "You saw Grady last night?"

Gin laughed at Suzanne's unspoken suggestion and handed her an extra pen. "He telephoned very early this morning, Suzanne."

"Oh, too bad." Suzanne's grin widened. "Now I'll never know if his rating's accurate."

"You're impossible, Suzanne!" Gin laughed outright. "If I'm not careful you'll have the gossips discussing *me*." She shook her head. "Go ahead and get started. I'll be right in."

Gin walked toward Mrs. Brashler's office, still chuckling over her co-worker's comments, then turned her thoughts to the holidays. If her request for leave was canceled, she'd have to call Aunt Millie tonight and say she wasn't coming. Disconsolately, she rapped on the door.

"Please sit down, Miss Selton." Mrs. Brashler indicated the chair across from her desk. "I'm sorry to say that I must deny your leave request." She held the holiday schedule in her hands. "You're low man on the totem pole, you know."

"I understand," Gin said, then smiled at the head nurse. "I just thought it wouldn't hurt to try. My aunt thinks I need to be with some family this Christmas. This is the first holiday without my parents, you know." She paused. "Actually, maybe it'll be better if I do work. The patients will take my mind off my own misery," she concluded, anxious to get back to her work.

Mrs. Brashler held up her hand. "Don't leave yet, Miss Selton. There's something else I want to discuss with you."

Slightly confused, Gin looked at the head nurse, and obediently sat back down.

"Mrs. St. John is doing well today, you know," Mrs. Brashler began.

"That's great! I'm glad we managed to save her."

"I must compliment you on the way you handled her critical condition, Miss Selton." Mrs. Brashler placed the schedule aside and folded her hands on her desk. "But unfortunately, Dr. Grady and I both feel you stepped out of bounds when you called him in."

"I needed help, Mrs. Brashler, and as usual Dr. Michaels was unavailable." Gin was surprised that Grady had seen the head nurse already. "I happened to know where Grady—uh, Dr. Grady—was."

"Well, Dr. Grady was most upset when he learned Dr. Michaels had informed you earlier that he would be in the interns' quarters. In any case, there are other doctors who should be called before disturbing Dr. Grady, my dear."

"Michaels wasn't around last night," Gin stated emphatically, trying to defend her actions.

"And you disobeyed your supervisor's direct orders." Mrs. Brashler went on. "I hate to say this, Miss Selton, because I'm sure you're an excellent nurse, but I think the stress of this unit may be affecting your judgment. I hope you don't mind, but I took the liberty of talking to the director of nurses today. There's an opening in Postpartum, and she's willing to let you transfer there after the first of the year."

Mrs. Brashler paused and arched her eyebrows at Gin. "We really feel this move will be good for you, Miss Selton. It's not the first time you've become too involved with your patients, you know. We're well aware of your recent personal problems. It's not easy to lose your parents and break off a romance within a few short weeks." Mrs. Brashler smiled sympathetically at Gin. "It will also be good for the unit. Here in Neuro, we must adhere strictly to hospital protocol."

Gin sat staring at Mrs. Brashler, not quite believing what was happening to her. Now she regretted having been so candid during her preemployment interview. Obviously they intended to use her past against her. "Postpartum?" she finally breathed.

"Yes. It's a fine unit. Lots of happy mothers and healthy babies. I think you'll learn to relax there, my dear, and it will give you an opportunity to expand your nursing skills."

"Grady spoke to you?" Gin clenched her fists, digging her nails into her hands.

"At length. He wanted me to stress the fact that your flagrant violation of the rules limiting your position is the reason he's so adamant about this transfer, but he did compliment your quick reactions."

Mrs. Brashler smiled again and pushed her chair away from the desk. "I feel much better now that this is over, Miss Selton. Frankly, I had some trepidations about our little chat." She looked at her watch. "Oh! You're late for report."

Gin obediently started to rise, then sat back down. She looked at Mrs. Brashler and frowned. "You know, Mrs. Brashler"—Gin crossed her legs and stared down at her white shoes—"I was in the grocery store the other day. I noticed how happy the checker seemed." She looked up again at the head nurse. "She didn't rush around the store, and she's going to be off for both holidays. I seriously doubt if in the entire time she's worked there she's had any sort of emergency arise—except that maybe the computer that rings the prices occasionally shuts down."

Mrs. Brashler nervously shuffled papers on her desk. "Yes, Miss Selton. Checkers do seem to have a rather nice job."

"Uh-huh, they do." Gin nodded in agreement. "They work eight hours, rarely punch out late, get an hour for lunch and two fifteen-minute breaks. And

you know, they make almost as much money as I do."
Gin rose, took off her name tag, and placed it on Mrs.
Brashler's desk. "All in all, it's a very attractive job."
She turned to leave.

"Miss Selton!" Mrs. Brashler called as Gin was
about to open the door. "Do you realize that if you
leave the unit like this your record will reflect your
disregard for the patients?"

Gin paused, her hand on the doorknob. "Mrs.
Brashler, you just accused me of becoming too involved with my patients."

"Don't leave the unit uncovered, Miss Selton."
Mrs. Brashler rounded the desk.

"Are you worried about who'll pull Christmas and
New Year's?" Gin grinned at the head nurse. "Do you
always allow your senior residents so much nursing
authority?"

"I've worked with temperamental interns and residents for years," Mrs. Brashler replied. "I find that
my life is ultimately easier if I comply with their
wishes."

"I thought so," Gin said. "See you at the grocery
store, Mrs. Brashler. Happy holidays."

As Gin walked out, she stuck her head in the report
room. "Meet me for lunch tomorrow, Suzanne.
Hardy's Coffee Shop at eleven," she added when Suzanne's mouth dropped open.

chapter 3

GIN PUSHED the salad around on her plate, then finally placed her fork on the table. "I'm sorry about last night," she said. She looked up at Suzanne. "Did they send you help?"

Suzanne nodded. "A nurse from the float pool and two extra aides." She shrugged. "It wasn't too bad."

Gin smiled at Suzanne's flippant attitude. "Did the float pool nurse work out all right?" It must have been awful, and she felt terrible about having left her friend to cope on her own.

"Yes. Well, Mr. Murphy didn't like her much." She giggled. "He shuffled all the way to the station with his walker to tell me she didn't know what a touchback was." She shook her head. "Tell you the truth, I don't know what it is either."

"Football term." Gin smiled at the image of Mr. Murphy struggling toward the nurses' station to complain about a football game. She shook her head in disbelief. "He's great!" she added. "I only hope he gets better."

"The radiation is going well," Suzanne offered.

"Is Mrs. Brashler making you work on Christmas?" Gin pushed her plate away and took a sip of coffee. She wasn't hungry.

Suzanne patted her rotund abdomen. "Well, with Junior on the way we can use the extra money. Besides, you just saved me from a fate worse than death."

Gin laughed. "What on earth could be worse than dinner in the hospital cafeteria?"

"Dinner with my mother-in-law."

"That bad, huh?" Gin leaned on the table, her chin in her hand, glad they were discussing Suzanne's problems instead of hers.

"She still thinks Robert is her sweet little boy instead of my very virile husband. I don't think she realizes we've conceived a child. Oh, no!" she groaned. "I just had a horrid thought."

"About your mother-in-law?" Gin laughed aloud at Suzanne's scowl. She hadn't known Suzanne for long, but she'd already realized that, despite her sometimes silly comments and giggling, Suzanne had a way of cutting to the heart of a subject.

Suzanne grimaced. "Next year I'll want to start my own Christmas traditions, and then I'll have to invite *her!* Ugh!" She laughed, then continued. "I shouldn't joke about her. She's really a nice lady, and I'm sure that when she has a grandchild to cuddle she'll be delightful." Suzanne finished her salad and eyed Gin's untouched plate.

Gin pushed the salad toward her. "You're going to be the size of a house by the time you deliver."

"Mmm, but food tastes so good these days!" Suzanne said, crunching on a celery stick. "Are you going home for the holidays now?"

"Don't I wish. I can't afford it now that I've quit my job."

"Those bills just keep piling up, don't they?" Suzanne's face lit up with sudden inspiration. "Hey, I'm off the Sunday before Christmas. Why don't you come for dinner? I can practice my culinary skills on you before I have to cook next year."

"I'd like that, but are you sure you'll be able to afford it? The way you're eating is incredible!"

"Any more bread sticks?" Suzanne glanced across the table, then sighed, leaning back in the booth. "What are you going to do now?" she asked.

"I applied at the National supermarket today." Gin added cream to the fresh coffee the waitress had poured her. "Thanks to Grady," she snapped angrily.

"You're leaving nursing?" Suzanne stared at her, aghast. "We've joked about it, but Gin, I don't believe that you of all people can just quit a profession that means so much to you."

"They wanted to transfer me to Postpartum. After the holidays, of course." Gin frowned. "I'd rather retire than listen to a bunch of women complain about their sore bottoms." She wrinkled her nose. "But I certainly would like to know what Noah Grady's got against me."

"Gin." Suzanne set her glass of milk down hard, almost spilling it. "You're probably not interested in my opinion, but I'm going to give it to you anyhow." Suzanne took a deep breath and stared thoughtfully at Gin. "I think Grady is *very* attracted to you."

"Suzanne, when did you have your prefrontal lobotomy? Or has the pregnancy messed up your mind, too?" Gin shook her head in disbelief.

Suzanne giggled, then immediately grew sober. "I'm serious, Gin," she insisted. "Don't you know how pretty you are?" She picked at a few cracker crumbs lying on her plate. "No," she continued, "I guess you don't. When you first came to Lakeside I hated you for having such a great figure. But you weren't at all snobbish about your looks, and you're the best nurse I've ever had the pleasure of working with."

Gin flushed in embarrassment. She'd had people tell her before how pretty she was, but she didn't see it herself. She was much too tall, and her facial features were too strong. Besides, blue-eyed blondes weren't exactly a rare commodity. "Do you have to be ugly to be a good nurse?" Gin asked, trying to hide her sudden discomfort.

"No, of course not!" Suzanne stated flatly. "But most young nurses at a medical center are only interested in one thing—catching a man."

"Well, a few of us around here happen to be interested in their careers." Gin laughed and began to search in her wallet for money.

"I'll get it, Gin. Thanks to you I'm going to need a Brink's truck to carry home my paycheck." Suzanne's eyes sparkled. "Anyhow, I think Grady's totally taken with you. You're very intelligent, you're pretty, and you've got the one thing most American men adore." Suzanne grinned broadly. "I had to get pregnant to know what it was like to have a man look at my chest."

Gin grimaced wryly. "If you're right, Suzanne, he has a strange way of showing it."

"You'd make a great couple, you know." Suzanne was bubbling with enthusiasm. "With your blond hair and blue eyes and his dark macho looks, think what great kids you'd produce."

"I hate to disappoint you, matchmaker friend of mine." Gin slid out of the booth, a smile tugging at her lips. "But despite Grady's good looks, I really wouldn't be interested in committing myself to feeding his ego, and I'm positive he isn't in the least interested in me."

"I still think I'm right," Suzanne insisted, following her to the parking lot. "Before you came to Lakeside, he hardly ever showed up in the evenings. Lately he's been there night after night, always with an excuse to see you or talk to you. Haven't you noticed the way he looks at you? The guy's just dying to get you into bed."

"Terrific! Are you recommending a romp in the hay with Noah Grady? What kind of friend are you, Suzanne?"

"He's just not sure how to approach you after that disastrous first encounter, Gin. It's difficult for the almighty Dr. Grady to admit he's wrong." Suzanne groaned, then rubbed her stomach. "I ate so much I can barely move. Anyhow, as I was saying, you don't exactly encourage men, you know. You're very cold and aloof when the other doctors are around. It's only when Grady appears that the sparks fly. I think you like him more than you care to admit."

Gin laughed aloud at Suzanne's suggestion. "Are you suggesting a love-hate relationship?"

"There's a fine line, Gin. I'm saying you and Grady are both denying your feelings."

"Thanks, Suzanne, for an inspirational lunch," Gin said as they got into their cars. "But as for men, doctors in particular, no thanks! I was crazy enough to be engaged to an obstetrician once, and believe me, one doctor was enough!"

Driving home, Gin reviewed their conversation. Suzanne had certainly come up with some irrational presumptions, and it amused Gin to realize her friend actually thought she might be interested in Noah Grady. The truth was that she'd left her profession because of him!

She had to admit, though, that it wasn't entirely because of Grady. She had been frustrated for a long time with the restrictions placed on her as a nurse.

Noah Grady had just pushed her beyond the limit of endurance.

She remembered her numerous, unfortunate encounters with Grady and realized how much his personality resembled her former fiancé's. Nick's overbearing attitude had made her life as miserable as had his unfaithfulness, she thought bitterly. For some reason, with or without emotional involvement, she seemed to attract hostile, arrogant men.

She sighed as she steered the car through a maze of heavy traffic. Had she made the right decision by leaving nursing so impetuously? Would she regret her rash behavior later? Or would a new perspective bring peace and order to her life? She hoped so, because her life was certainly in a state of chaos now.

"I'm coming, just a minute!" Gin shouted at the persistent doorbell. She flipped off the television set. "I'm coming!" she yelled again when the buzzer continued its irritating summons.

She threw open the door, already angry at the person standing outside, but instead of uttering a berating remark, Gin gaped foolishly at Noah Grady. He stood in the doorway with annoying nonchalance, looking better in Gin's opinion than anyone with such a detestable character had a right to look.

Grady pointed to the file card he was holding. "It says here your name is Ginelle. I didn't know that." He let his eyes roam slowly down her body in a long, appreciative inspection.

"Now you know. What the hell do you want, Grady?" Gin narrowed her eyes at him.

"You're hard to find, Selton. You changed your phone number. Suzanne Bonati refuses to talk to me, and Mrs. Brashler just stalks off when I ask about you. I finally had to bribe some turkey in Personnel to pull your records. It ended up costing me fifty bucks." He glared back at her as if it were her fault. "He said you were terminated."

"The turkey was right!" Gin said. "Good-bye, Grady." Gin started to slam the door, but he managed to push it further open.

"Then where the hell are you working? I called Westland and City General, and you weren't on either neuro unit."

"It's none of your business, Grady, but I start at the National next week." Gin started to close the door again. "Now if you'll excuse me."

Grady stopped the door with his hand and stared at her, his eyebrows furrowed. He was so close Gin could smell the faint odor of his musky after-shave, and when she looked up at him, his gray eyes were the color of molten steel.

"When are you moving to Washington?" he asked finally.

"Grady, you're positively brilliant!" Gin folded her arms and smiled smugly at him. "Don't you eat?"

"What?" Grady ran a hand through his unruly dark hair. For once he seemed at a loss for words. "What's that got to do with it?"

"National Food Stores?" Gin leaned against the door frame, still smiling patiently at him. "Sound familiar?"

"You're working at a *food store?*" Grady exclaimed.

Their voices had attracted several other tenants in Gin's apartment building, who were standing in their doorways listening to their noisy exchange. Grady glanced at their fascinated audience.

"Let me in," he ordered.

"This isn't the hospital, Grady," Gin fumed. "You aren't God here! Get out of my apartment!"

she said as he pushed her inside and slammed the door closed.

"Call me Noah," he ordered. "Grady sounds like a curse when you say it."

Gin sighed with frustration. "Look, Grady. I'm not up to another verbal exchange with you. Will you please tell me what you want from me and then get out of my apartment?"

"Right now, I want to know why the hell you're leaving nursing," Grady shouted, gesticulating wildly. He seemed to fill her apartment with angry energy.

"You and Mrs. Brashler wanted me to transfer to Postpartum. That's not my field, so I decided to try something a bit more congenial." Gin sat down on the sofa, her arms folded defiantly, and glared at him. "This may surprise you, but a person doesn't have to be male to possess intelligence," she spat. "You don't want nurses on your unit, Grady, you want hand-maidens who believe you're as infallible as you do. Nursing has advanced from those days, or at least *I* have."

"What do you expect from the world, Ginny Selton? What do you expect from me?" Grady stood over her, shouting even louder, and Gin looked sharply up at him.

Nick was the only other person who had ever called her Ginny. Grady had no right! "What gives you the idea you can come here and question me, Grady? You're the one who made my life miserable at Lakeside!"

"Look, Selton." Grady's eyes contained a mockery intended to make her feel inferior. "You can't change the world. There are certain things in life that can't be reversed—ever!" Grady's jaw was clenched, and a muscle jumped in his cheek.

"I can try, Grady!" Gin sprang up from the sofa

and faced him, her head tossed back defiantly.

"That's right." He glared down at her. "I forgot, nobody dies on Selton's shift."

"Not if I can help it!" she shot back. "The night of my parents' accident I helplessly watched them die while the emergency-room staff debated about calling in another doctor. I swore then that would never happen as long as I had anything to do with the profession. I apologize for disturbing your night of fornication with the lovely nurse from Intensive Care. That's what's bothering you, isn't it? It's not my qualifications or my motivations!"

"No!" Grady grabbed her arms and pulled her close. His eyes sparkled with fury—and with something else that frightened her. "That's not what's bothering me! What the hell have you got against men, and against me in particular?"

"Nothing earth-shattering, Grady." Gin tried to pull away from his grip. She could feel his heart pounding so close to her own, and her pulse quickened in response. The warmth of his hand penetrated the material covering her arm as if branding her with his touch.

"Noah!" he said through clenched teeth. "The name is Noah."

"I just can't tolerate egotistical physicians!" she exclaimed. "And you're the most conceited one I've ever had the displeasure to meet!"

"That's right!" His cheek was twitching again. "I am cocky, but what you don't realize is that you're just as proud where your profession is concerned as I am. I swear, I've never met a woman as frustrating as you are!"

When she stood her ground without wavering, Grady released her arms, then ran his hand through his hair again. "You're not going to change a system that's thousands of years old, Ginny. You can't practice medicine without a license."

"Grady—Noah"—she corrected in response to his scowl—"I hate to continue this disagreement, but I was strictly within bounds. You're the one who has tried to make me look foolish all these weeks. Why did you report me to Mrs. Brashler? Answer that!"

"Because someone had to stop you—"

"No!" Gin lashed out before he could finish. "Don't try to lie to me! Your ego just can't tolerate the fact that I know what I'm doing and that several times I've been right."

"All right," he said, narrowing his eyes, "I'll buy that. I'll even admit it may be the truth. But since we're examining motives, suppose you tell me why you put on the deep freeze when I'm around."

Gin sat down on the sofa again, then wearily indicated a chair. She tossed her long blond hair over her shoulders and sighed deeply. She didn't want to tell him about Nick, but how else was she going to get rid of him? And she was more and more desperate to do just that—to get him out of her apartment and out of her life before something terrible happened. He was just too dangerous to have around.

"All right," she began. "This is also none of your business, but maybe you'll leave me alone if I tell you." She paused, folding her hands in her lap. She found self-revelation of any sort difficult, but perhaps he did deserve the truth. She wondered, however, if it would do any good, if it would make him leave.

"I was in love with a doctor like you once," she began again, then her voice trailed off. "I can't seem to forget..." She shifted uncomfortably on the sofa, then continued with forced indifference. "You remind me a lot of him. You've got the same winning personality, only he was an obstetric resident." She looked up at him, smiling at her attempt at a joke, but his silvery eyes were riveted to her face, taking her breath away. She swallowed with difficulty before going on. "I heard the nasty rumors, but I didn't believe any of them. I faced my co-workers every day, knowing they were gossiping about me. I-I didn't care." She sighed, allowing herself to remember, then blushed and averted her eyes when she once again met his probing gaze. "Anyhow, when my parents died after that terrible car accident, I needed him. I went to his apartment and found him with another nurse."

Grady leaned back in the chair and stretched his long legs out, crossing his hands behind his head. She could almost feel the tension leaving his body, and his voice was soft when he said, "None of that explains why you avoid me as if I had a dread disease."

"Your reputation has preceded you, Grady," she told him. "Perhaps I took my anger at Nick out on you and I'm sorry if that's so, but I don't intend to be in that situation ever again."

Grady stared at her for a long moment, then abruptly rose from the chair. "Get dressed," he ordered.

"What?" Gin stared at him.

"Now you're the brilliant one." Grady smiled, his eyes crinkling at the corners, making his face light up with warmth. "Get dressed, and leave your hair down. It looks pretty that way. You remind me of a nun with your hair in that twist or whatever it's called."

"I don't believe you, Grady. Will you just please leave me alone. I'm not interested in talking with you." Suddenly this nicer Noah Grady seemed even more threatening to her than his less friendly alter ego.

"N-o-a-h," Grady corrected patiently once again, still grinning at her. "And no conversation. You're absolutely right. I have been unfair, and I intend to make amends. At the very least I owe you a good dinner."

"You don't owe me anything, G—Noah." Gin shook her head. "And quite frankly, they'd probably throw us out of a restaurant the moment we opened our mouths. I don't think we can talk to each other without screaming."

"Tell you what, Ginny. If I shout, or even so much as raise my voice tonight, you can kick me under the table."

"Not severe enough punishment," Gin asserted. "And please don't call me Ginny."

"Well, *Ginny*"—Grady plopped down in a chair—"cook something then. I'm hungry."

"I'm not going to cook for you, nor am I going to tolerate you for another minute. Get out!" Gin's voice started to rise again.

"Okay, Selton." Grady's voice took on a teasing tone, but with a hint of underlying steel. "You've got a choice. Either you get dressed and eat dinner with me tonight, or I'll give your name and number to the hospital operator and tell her to forward all my calls here for the night."

"You wouldn't!" Gin's eyes sparked with anger.

"You don't like gossip, do you?" Grady remarked calmly as he headed toward the telephone.

"No! Don't!" Gin said. Wide-eyed, she stared at him. "You're really rotten, you know."

Giving up, Gin headed for the bedroom and slammed the door shut behind her. She leaned against it for a moment, trying to calm herself, then blushed when she noticed her reflection in the dresser mirror.

She had forgotten she was wearing the satin loung-

ing pajamas her mother, of all people, had given her
for her birthday. Low-necked and revealing, they were
meant to be seductive. The high swell of her breasts
was exposed, and anger had flushed her skin a rosy
pink. The lush fabric clung to her hips and thighs in
an alluring manner.

She stripped, angry that he had seen her this way
and angrier still that she had confided in him. She
hastily pulled on a pair of slacks and a bulky sweater,
drew a brush through her hair, and applied a dab of
lipstick. When she reentered the room, Grady was on
the phone talking to his answering service.

"Very nice," he said when he replaced the telephone, his eyes raking boldly over her body. "But I
much prefer you in the other outfit."

"Look, Grady." Gin clenched her hands at her
sides. "I'm not going to jump into bed with you, no
matter what you threaten me with. So if that's what
you're leading up to, I can save you the trouble of
trying."

"I came here tonight because I was concerned about
what—"

"Grady," she cut in, "you may have come here for
a variety of reasons, but concern wasn't one of them."

Grady held his hands up in mock innocence. "No
strings," he said, a smile tugging at his lips. "I'm not
often humble, Ginny, but you're absolutely right. I
was rotten to you those weeks at Lakeside. But I can
try to make it up to you."

"You're getting away cheap, Noah, if you think
dinner can make up for all the misery you've put me
through." Gin grabbed her coat and purse.

"No strings, I promise, Ginny," he repeated, then
paused, grinning a charming, lopsided smile that made
Gin's heart make strange flip-flops. "For now, anyway."

chapter 4

THE NEXT DAY Gin still found it hard to believe she'd consented to spend an evening with Noah Grady, even if he had blackmailed her. She let the sharp needles of the shower beat down on her aching shoulders, feeling herself relax in the invigorating spray. She shampooed her long hair, scrubbed her scalp, and wished that *something* would help ease the headache she'd had since last night. She knew it was caused by tension and built-up anger. First the screaming match with Noah Grady had upset her, then dinner had been an emotional disaster.

At first they had both tried to avoid any subjects that might set off a spat, and consequently there were many long moments of tense silence. Gin had been so distraught by the intimate atmosphere of the restaurant and the abrupt change in Grady's attitude toward her that now she couldn't remember what she'd eaten. The plush velvet booths had helped create a private, intimate nook perfect for seduction, while the single candle that flickered in the crimson vase, high-lighting the chiseled features of Noah's handsome face, had added to the romantic atmosphere.

Noah had ordered for her in his usual forceful manner, ignoring her request to choose her own dishes, and then he'd insisted they toast to their futures.

To cover her discomfort at finding herself so physically close to this arrogant man who irritated her to no end—and not being able to do anything about it—Gin drank too much white wine and began talking nervously.

Later, after Noah had badgered her into eating all the food on her plate—she had to admit his choices had been excellent—he began to discuss the possibility of her returning to Lakeside. Gin flatly refused to consider his suggestion, and when it seemed they might clash again, she bit her tongue to keep from uttering a sarcastic, flippant remark he might misinterpret. She had spent a restless, sleepless night, then this morning at dawn had started to clean her small apartment furiously. Every inch of the place was polished and shiny, but the hard work hadn't relieved her tension.

She stepped out of the shower, towel-dried her hair, and slipped into the pale blue silk robe she'd impulsively purchased that day. V-necked and floor-length, it had tiny pearl buttons down the front beginning just where her breasts began to swell. A wide velvet ribbon in deep blue circled her slim waist.

Gin turned from side to side, enjoying the sensuous swish of the fabric against her bare skin. The robe was an extravagance, but she'd needed something to lift her spirits. Wriggling her nose at her image in the mirror, Gin vowed to save her pennies from now on until she started work again.

Gin wandered into the kitchen and rummaged through the contents of the refrigerator. Already she was bored, and she didn't start work for another week. Resolutely, she closed the door on the tempting food inside, went back into the living room, and turned on the television. Flipping the channels impatiently, she finally tuned in the familiar voice of a well-known sports announcer.

Ignoring her vow—made only moments before—to diet faithfully, Gin went back into the kitchen and made a huge bowl of popcorn, then poured a diet cola. The smell of the popcorn reminded her of many pleasant evenings she'd shared with her folks and of the huge bowls of it they'd eaten during football games. Suddenly she felt desolately alone. She concentrated on the banter of the announcers, trying to forget the pain of her parents' death. Along with everything else, the past few months had taught her how to wipe all conscious thought from her mind.

She was making her way back into the living room when she heard the buzzing of the doorbell. Juggling her popcorn and drink in one hand, Gin opened the door, then stared dumfounded at Noah Grady. He was standing in the hall, his hands thrust deep into his trouser pockets, and she noticed without really thinking about it that his shoulders were almost as wide as her doorway.

"I guess it won't do much good to tell you I don't want your company tonight," she said, surprised to hear the testiness in her voice.

"None at all," he said, flashing her an offhand grin. "It's cold out there!" he exclaimed as he swept into the room uninvited.

"It *is* winter, Grady." Shaking her head, but realizing it was useless to protest, Gin closed the door behind him. "What do you want tonight?" she asked when he'd shed his heavy coat and gloves.

Noah's cheeks were ruddy, and he blew on his hands to warm them. Vaguely Gin noticed how strong and supple his hands were.

He flashed her another quick, lopsided grin, making her realize she was staring senselessly at him. Then he noticed the popcorn and took the bowl from her hands. The contact of his hands on hers startled her, making her jerk away. "You still haven't forgiven me," he said. "I intend to make amends."

"You're forgiven. Now what?" Gin stood still before him, not able to think clearly and terribly aware of the revealing robe she was wearing.

Even the air in the room seemed charged with electricity as his eyes took in every inch of her appearance, lingering at the deep V of her neckline. As if with supreme effort, he finally tore his eyes away and turned to the television set. "Football game on tonight?"

"It's a Thursday night special," she explained when she could once again command her lips to move. "Oilers versus Browns."

Grady plopped into a chair, and Gin sat down on the sofa across from him, carefully closing the slit in her robe over her bare thighs. Everything in her experience shouted that this was a very dangerous situation, yet she felt riveted to the seat, her legs too weak to take her into the bedroom to change, her voice closed against the words she knew she ought to say to make him leave. Without anger to protect her, she was mesmerized by his very presence.

Finally she heard her voice as if from a distance and wondered if it were really hers. "I'm not going to fall for your act, Grady," she said. "I thought I made it clear last night I'm not interested in a relationship with you." There, she had voiced the suspicions pounding in her brain.

"Even if I promise not to ravish you, Ginny?" Noah grinned at her again, throwing handfuls of popcorn into his mouth, but her name sounded like a caress when he said it. "Scout's honor." He held his hand to his forehead in a mock salute.

"You were never a Boy Scout, Grady." Gin glared at him in an effort to regain her senses. He was making her distinctly uncomfortable, even though he was acting as if they were casual friends.

"Noah," he corrected.

"Noah!" Gin shot back impatiently.

"And I *was* a Boy Scout," he continued, as if it really mattered. "I never made it past first class, though."

"Noah." Gin tried desperately to hold her mounting anger in check. "I can't take another screaming match with you. My head is still killing me from last night."

At his brief look of clinical concern, Gin shook her head. "No, Noah, you don't have another potential craniotomy here. It's tension."

Noah placed the bowl of popcorn on the coffee table, then rounded the sofa to stand behind Gin. For some reason he seemed taller and more masculine than she remembered, and that thought made her even more uneasy. Before she could object, he placed his hands on her shoulders and began to massage them, his fingers digging into the tense muscles of her neck.

"Please don't," Gin murmured, trying to pull away, but his strong hands pushed her back into the sofa. "Please, Noah." Again she tried to escape his hands.

"Do you like football? I can change the channel," Noah said, his voice as smooth as glass as he continued to ply her shoulder muscles. He moved his hands further down her back over the silky blue fabric, and Gin squirmed, trying to avoid his probing fingers and the alarming sensations they were arousing.

"It's my television, Grady!" she finally snapped. "And yes, I like football. Now will you *please* stop!"

"Not until your headache is gone." Noah pulled her shoulders back and massaged harder, moving up to her neck, the sensuous gesture sending shivers along her spine.

"It's gone, I swear!" Gin moved again, trying to escape his sensitive hands. His touch was sending tiny tingles of electricity all over her body, and she uttered another protest, then twisted hard from his grip and stood up. "Please don't touch me," she whispered, realizing she was trembling visibly.

Deliberately ignoring her plea, Grady walked around the sofa and came to stand just inches away from her, his distinctive male scent assailing her nostrils. "What's the matter, Ginny? Can't you deny your attraction to me when I'm touching you?" He ran a finger down the length of her arm, and the magnetism between them was almost tangible.

Gin's unease changed to panic in the interminable moment, and she spoke angrily at him. "This may be a shock to your ego, Grady, but some women are easily able to resist your charm."

"And you're one of them?" His eyebrow was cocked disbelievingly, and his low voice sent another shiver of apprehension through her.

When she didn't answer, Grady strode back to his chair and picked up the popcorn. "It's unusual for a woman to like football." He held the bowl toward her as if they were casually chatting about the weather. "Popcorn?"

Growing more exasperated with him, and with her incomprehensible response to him, Gin shook her head. She had never met a man as mercurial as Noah Grady, nor one who could irritate her so quickly. "Are you claiming to be an expert on the entire female gender, now?" she asked, her tone derisive.

"I'll bet you were a cheerleader. Got another Coke?" He looked expectantly at her, as if there weren't an incredible tension between them, and Gin seethed at his ability to hide the emotions she was fighting so desperately. "No, I don't have another Coke!" Her voice was perilously close to a scream, and she started with surprise when Grady lunged from his chair and clamped his hand over her mouth.

"I just want to be friends," he said, slowly and distinctly. "That's all. Now, if you really don't want to get into another screaming match, can I get my own Coke?"

"I'll get it," Gin said when he released his hand, rising from the sofa. "I suppose you want some more popcorn, too," she muttered, glancing at the empty bowl.

Gin could hear Grady cheering at the television set as she emptied a new batch of popcorn into the bowl. It aggravated her to think he could dominate her so easily, that he was sitting in her living room against her will. She sprinkled extra salt onto the kernels with malicious glee. I hope he dies of thirst, she thought, then realized how childishly she was behaving. If she really wanted him out of her apartment—and her life—she would just have to make it clear he wasn't welcome.

"The Browns just caught a forty-yard touchdown pass," Grady said when she reentered the room. "I'm an Oilers fan, but out of deference to our agreement I'll cheer for whatever team you like."

"How considerate of you." Gin arched her eyebrow at him, the opportunity to utter a scathing remark making her momentarily abandon her vow to confront him. She purposely focused her attention on the television screen. She would *not* let him spoil another evening!

They watched the game in comparative silence, commenting occasionally on a play or asking for the popcorn. But despite Noah's friendlier attitude, Gin could not fully relax in his presence. When the game was over, Noah looked at his watch, then pointedly back at her. "Three hours without a single argument," he said with a quick grin.

"A world record," Gin commented dryly. Although she had tried to concentrate on the game, she hadn't the vaguest idea what had happened. The only thing she was sure of was that she desperately wanted him to leave. Obviously she would have to resort to rudeness to rid herself of his presence. "It's late," she said, throwing him a meaningful look. "Don't you have surgery in the morning?"

"I require very little sleep," Noah shrugged, his expression making her aware of *other* things done at night. "Habit left over from medical school. Do you mind if I call in?"

"Why don't you just leave?" Gin suggested, then sighed at his threatening look and waved him toward the phone. An awkward silence followed in the wake of the magnetic tension between them, making her even more nervous. "Want some coffee?" she finally asked. Noah nodded as he dialed the number. Gin heard his muffled voice from the kitchen, and as she carried steaming mugs of coffee into the living room, she heard him recite her number.

"Don't worry," he said as he hung up, grining mischievously at her, obviously knowing she had overheard. "They won't give your number out, especially after last week. I just thought it might be more convenient than calling in every few hours."

"You're not staying that long, Noah," Gin told him sarcastically, "so don't make any plans. We may have gotten through a few hours without coming to blows, but I'm still not interested in a casual romp in the sack."

"I must have a very bad reputation." Noah's eyes crinkled, making her aware that he knew very well what his reputation was. He turned abruptly and walked over to the window with his mug of coffee. Peering between the draperies, he looked down at the empty street. Tiny flakes of snow swirled down, covering with white, glittering diamonds the candy canes, holly wreaths, and plastic Santas that decorated the houses. "Are you going home for Christmas?" he asked as he let the drapes fall back into place.

"I can't afford to now." Gin shook her head. "I've got just enough money to cover the rent and my car payment. I splurged on a turkey and the ingredients for a bowl of wassail today. I think I'll just relax for a change. In the past I've always had to work."

"Do you need some extra money?" Noah asked.

Gin bristled at his implication, then caught herself when she realized he was merely being polite. "No." She laughed and indicated her robe. "As long as I can spend my hard-earned dollars on foolish items like this, I should pay penance for a few weeks."

Gin looked down at her gaping robe, then quickly drew it tightly closed. She should have changed into slacks, she thought again. But to do so now might make Noah think she was aware of him as a desirable man. She noticed with a sinking feeling that he was staring at her again, as if he could see through the rich fabric, and she felt suddenly naked and vulnerable.

"W-what are you doing for Christmas?" Gin stuttered, trying to think of any subject that might draw his attention away from her body.

"I gave my residents the week off." Grady returned

to his chair and grinned at her. "Until Mrs. St. John ruptured, I was planning to have dinner with Mary Anne Harner."

Gin nibbled nervously at her lower lip, then stopped when she realized his gaze was now resting on her full mouth. "That's my fault," she said. "Look, why don't I call her and tell her I'm sorry."

Noah shook his head. "Wouldn't do any good. She thinks we're having a torrid affair.

"You're kidding!" Gin laughed. "Us?"

"The thought isn't that incredible." Grady said, his soft gray eyes alight with something Gin wasn't prepared to name. "She thinks we're covering up for the benefit of the gossips. Actually, I think I like her suggestion." His voice was once again low and husky.

Gin flushed but pretended she didn't hear his final comment. "Are you sure you don't want me to call her?" she asked briskly, trying to appear relaxed.

"She was a casual companion, Ginny. Nothing more. Truthfully, your phone call didn't spoil a meaningful relationship." Grady gave a short half laugh and, finishing his coffee, set the cup on the table. "I've managed to evade meaningful relationships. And anyway, I hear Dr. Michaels has canceled his trip and is filling my shoes adequately."

"Well, you can always eat Christmas dinner in the hospital cafeteria." Gin tried to sound flippant and unconcerned, finally remembering what their conversation had originally been about. She shifted nervously and tucked her feet under her. She was having trouble holding her robe closed and juggling her coffee while trying to appear comfortable.

Noah watched her squirm on the sofa, then grimaced. "They don't serve pasta with dinner," he said, his eyes dropping to the expanse of thigh she had accidentally exposed.

"What?" Gin said, wrinkling her brow in puzzlement and quickly closing her robe when she noticed the direction of his stare.

"Ravioli, mostaccioli, spaghetti." He grinned. "I'm half Italian, you know."

"And on Christmas you have pasta?"

"Every Sunday and twice during the week, too." Noah patted his taut abdomen. "Very fattening food."

"You'd never know it, looking at you." Gin stared at his lean, muscular body. For a moment she felt a totally inconsistent urge to reach out and touch him.

"Oh, really?" he said softly, and when she realized he knew what she had been thinking, her face flamed. Mortified that he had read her thoughts, she shifted uneasily and stifled a yawn.

"That tired? It would certainly be a blow to my ego to think I'm boring you." Noah leaned back, clasping his hands behind his head as he studied her intently. He kept his gaze riveted to the slight curve of her breasts, as if he were waiting for her to drop her hold on the neckline of her robe.

"I didn't sleep well last night," Gin explained. "Unlike temperamental neurosurgeons, we nurses need our rest."

Noah studied her through hooded eyes for a moment, then stood and walked slowly toward her. The mockery that she had come to expect was gone from the gray eyes that were now so close to her own. She was acutely aware of his masculinity, and she felt her heart pound furiously when he reached out his hand to gently caress her cheek. "You're sure you want me to leave?" He smiled gently down at her, then placed his hands on her shoulders and let them slide down the length of the soft, silky fabric. "Surely you aren't going to deny the physical attraction between us."

Gin was all too aware of how devastatingly attractive he was, but she shoved the thought quickly to the back of her mind. He was an egotistical rogue, she reminded herself, who wasn't in the least interested in her feelings. He was another Nick Carlin—although perhaps a bit more attractive and suave—and he would only hurt her if she let herself become emotionally involved. Noah Grady would never make a commitment. Wasn't one unfaithful man enough?

Gin quickly extricated herself from his encircling arms, then jumped up and grabbed his jacket. She handed it to him, hoping her shaking hands wouldn't betray her. "I'm quite sure I want you to leave, Noah," she said briskly.

He smiled ruefully and shrugged into his coat. Pausing at the door, he looked searchingly at her. For one fleeting second she watched an indefinable emotion flare up in his eyes, and then it was gone so swiftly she thought she must have imagined it.

"Merry Christmas, Ginny," he said huskily, then turned abruptly and left.

Gin closed the door behind him and leaned weakly against it. She was certain he wouldn't return, especially after the way she'd discouraged his advances. A man like Noah Grady didn't waste time on unwilling women. She admitted she was relieved. His presence bothered her, and she knew deep down that she was attracted to him—more than she would ever care to admit.

She grinned, thinking of Suzanne's predictions. In a way her friend had been right, but Gin had no intention of furthering this relationship! All Noah Grady could give her would be physical pleasure. If she ever committed herself to another man, it would be someone who would cherish her, not some egotistical doctor who thrilled her with his touch.

"Good-bye, Noah Grady," Gin whispered, then sighed and headed toward the bathroom.

chapter 5

GIN SPREAD marshmallows on top of the sweet potatoes and put them into the oven, then turned to the
arduous task of making gravy. It took an accomplished
cook to make a big meal, she thought to herself,
remembering the many scrumptious dinners her mother
had prepared on previous holidays. She brushed away
a tear that had slipped down her cheek. It wouldn't
do any good to think of the past or of her parents, she
reasoned. But she felt so lonely today. She should
have gone to Aunt Mil's house for Christmas despite
her straitened finances.

She turned back to the gravy, stirring vigorously
when bubbles appeared in the skillet, then started with
surprise at the sound of the doorbell.

"Go away," she yelled from the kitchen. "It's
Christmas!" The number of salespeople this apartment
building attracted always amazed her.

"Nobody's home!" she shouted again when the
buzzer continued to sound. "If you're some kid selling

candy, I'm going to scream," she muttered. Realizing that whoever was at the door wasn't going away, she shut off the burners, wiped her hands on the makeshift apron she was wearing, and headed for the living room.

Gin opened the door and blinked in disbelief. Noah Grady filled the doorway, a bowl balanced precariously in one hand, a small pine tree sticking out from under his arm at a jaunty angle, and a big grin on his face. His neck was draped with a long Christmas garland, and melting snowflakes clung to his dark hair.

"Noah!" Gin cried when she finally regained her senses. "What are you doing here?"

He swept into the room, smiling conspiratorially at her, and shoved the bowl into her hands while shrugging out of his jacket. "I slaved over these ravioli all morning, and they're getting cold while you give me the third degree."

Gin fought a sudden, almost irresistible urge to brush the glittering snow from his hair and turned quickly away. "You made these?" she asked, indicating the bowl of pasta.

"As incredible as it sounds, my folks always thought I'd become a chef. I was the youngest in my family and used to help my mother cook for the six other kids. Ravioli was our favorite and her specialty. Am I too late for dinner?"

"No," Gin said, staring up into his eyes and realizing suddenly she couldn't let him stay. "I was just finishing everything, but—"

"Good, I'm starved," Noah interrupted. "Got another plate?"

"We can't spend Christmas together," Gin objected quickly.

"Why not?" He grinned at her, that charming, crooked smile that made her pulse quicken. "We're both alone."

Gin wanted to say, because I'm not sure I can resist you any longer and I don't want to be hurt again, but she just kept shaking her head.

"Where's that bowl of wassail you were going to make?" He looked around, once again ignoring her protests as inconsequential. "It's freezing out there. Big snowstorm blowing in."

Gin continued to shake her head as he propped the pine tree in the corner. "I can't let you stay, Noah," she objected again, making her voice sound firm.

"We need some decorations." He stepped back to view the tree, examining it critically from all sides. "Got some hair ribbons?"

Ignoring his question Gin sniffed the air suspiciously. "Oh, no!" she cried. "The marshmallows are burning!" She ran to rescue the sweet potatoes, then, sighing, pulled another plate from the cabinet. Surely it wouldn't hurt to share one dinner with him. She admitted she was actually glad he had stopped by. Christmas was meant to be shared with other people. Not that she liked him any more than before. He was still the same conceited neurosurgeon who had a knack for irritating her, but he was right, they were both alone.

Gin lit a candle and placed platters of food on the festive table while Noah tied bright bows and hung the garland on the tree. He had tuned in a local radio station and was humming along with the holiday songs.

Gin listened to his deep, seductive voice as she fussed with dinner and wondered idly if he sang in the shower. Immediately she chided herself for thinking such a silly thing and focused her attention on the table, putting her conflicting feelings about Noah Grady out of her mind.

Noah finished decorating the tree and turned toward her. "Oh, I almost forgot." He reached into his pocket and held out a tiny package gaily wrapped in holiday paper, complete with a huge red bow. As he handed it to her with a flourish, his expression reminded Gin of a little boy who'd just accomplished a fantastic feat. "I brought you a present," he announced.

"Noah, we aren't exactly at the point of exchanging presents." Gin held the box in her hands, excited despite her words, but did not unwrap it. "I can't accept this."

"Didn't you get me anything?" he said with a crushed look.

"No, I didn't get you anything. I didn't think I'd ever see you again." Gin stared at him, remembering how easily he aroused her anger. Why did she let him irritate her so!

"Open it anyhow." Noah reached out and caressed her cheek, flashing that devastating smile. "I promise not to pout."

He was standing uncomfortably close to her, and Gin felt a magnetic attraction grow between them. For a moment she thought she would drown in the sheer intoxication of his presence. Moving quickly away she tried to collect her thoughts.

Focusing on the present, she tore off the wrappings hoping he hadn't noticed how badly her hands were shaking. When she finally opened the box, she stared for a moment at the contents. "A pocket flashlight?" She looked up at him.

"I thought you needed one," Noah explained. "The

night we met you were having trouble with yours, weren't you?"

"The batteries drive me crazy," Gin laughed. "They always go out at the most inappropriate times."

"Well, this is a very expensive flashlight. I got it at Neiman's."

She turned the slim silver tube over in her hand and noticed the engraved name on it. "This is a freebie from some drug company, Noah," Gin said laughing again. "But thank you anyway."

Noah grinned guiltily at her. "What did you expect from a poor, starving senior resident?" he chided. *"When* are we going to eat?"

"Just as soon as you tell me what I'm going to do with a flashlight. You know I've quit my job."

"Let's eat first. You're not going to like what I have to say about that." Noah poured two steaming mugs of wassail and handed her one.

"Noah, I'm *not* going back to Lakeside," Gin began, "so there's nothing to argue about."

"Why not?" he asked. "What are you afraid of? Or is it your wounded pride?"

"I'm not *afraid* of anything, Noah, and my pride— even though you were the one who wounded it—is none of your business."

"Then I'll pick you up tomorrow and we'll talk to Mrs. Brashler together. You can apologize, and I'll insist she give you back your position."

"No!" Gin shook her head and sipped the fragrant, spicy punch. Once again he assumed he could simply overrule her objections. The fact that he thought she would apologize for something she didn't do infuriated her. "After today I don't plan to see *you* ever again."

"Oh?" Noah moved closer to her and, despite her

anger, Gin felt as if every nerve in her body had come alive. He lifted his mug in a silent toast, and she tingled as tiny shock waves coursed through her. She was unprepared for the harsh bitterness of his words. "Then here's to Ginny Selton, quitter and coward," he said. "And I may as well add 'liar' to that list of virtues. You can't admit you were wrong, can you? You can't admit you quit the hospital because of your desire for me."

"You're incredible, Grady!" Gin snapped, her voice rising. "Now you've decided that I'm not only incompetent—as you have so pointedly insisted these last few weeks—but you've also decided I'm some sex-starved idiot just dying to make love to you. Well, I don't intend to listen to your demented ravings on Christmas Day. Get out of my apartment!"

"I don't care what day this is!" Noah retorted, his body becoming taut with anger. "It's about time someone showed you you're just as fallible as the rest of us humans." He put down his cup and began circling the table, his gray eyes flashing. "I admitted I was wrong. You're a damn good nurse, and I regret what happened at the hospital, but at least I . . ." He ran his hands through his hair in a gesture of impatience. "What the hell!" he spat. "I should just shake some sense into that thick, stubborn skull of yours."

Gin backed away as he strode toward her, unsure of his intention. "Don't you dare touch—" she started, then gasped as his hand grasped her wrist in an iron grip.

Before she realized what he was doing, he pulled her toward him, pressing her against the hard length of his body and kissing her, his lips harsh and demanding.

"No!" Gin cried against his mouth. She tried frantically to move her head, but he held it fast between his hands, entwining his fingers tightly in her long blond hair. His lips continued to bruise her soft mouth, seeking and claiming it for his own, plundering the moist depths.

She struggled desperately, fighting not only Noah but also the sudden onrush of fire he was stirring up in her treacherous body. She held herself stiffly, trying to deny the overwhelming urge to kiss him back, but desire spread like molten fire through her body. Her heart pounded in her ears, obliterating all other sounds.

"I've wanted to do that for so long," Noah whispered, his voice husky with passion. He crushed her against him, his hands no longer holding her head still, but now moving down her back as his lips met hers again in a flaming challenge.

She felt as if she were being swept up in a sudden raging storm she was helpless to fight. Her body was weakened further when his lips seared hers repeatedly, leaving her breathless, while his fingers caressed the curve of her throat.

She was surprised to feel her hands creep up over his shoulders. Her fingers ran hesitantly through his crisp hair, then down his back. An uncontrollable weakness seized her, and her legs wobbled and refused to support her as Noah continued his intoxicating assault on her senses. She slumped against him, limp and pliant.

"I want you, Ginny," he whispered in her ear, his breath tantalizing her. "And I know you want me."

Through a white-hot haze of passion she felt his hands inside her blouse, caressing the bare skin on her back, then coming around to brush ever so gently over her turgid breasts. An unbearable, overpowering desire throbbed through her veins, and she pressed hard against him.

She moaned, then shook her head slightly to try to clear it, to gather the strength to fight the onslaught of emotions he was arousing in her trembling body. But his hands were warm against her bare breasts, his fingers pressing and kneading the taut nipples, and she was unable to move away from the exquisite torture.

"Ginny?" he whispered again, and his voice was like a caress as he nuzzled her earlobe with his lips.

Gin sobbed, slumping against him, passion consuming her. God help her, he was right. She wanted him! With a tiny sigh she gave in totally to her feelings, nodding her head against his chest, then slipped her hands boldly inside his shirt, running her fingers over the taut muscles that rippled across his back as he held her tightly, caressing her.

She shivered when he peeled off her blouse, then grazed her bare shoulders with his lips. Wave after wave of exhilarating sensations coursed through her body as his lips traced another path from her mouth to her breast, his tongue flicking tantalizingly over her sensitive skin.

Noah swore softly, then picked her up and strode into the bedroom, kicking the door closed behind him. The finality of his gesture made Gin realize that there was no turning back, and she buried her face in his chest.

He placed her gently on the bed, then quickly stripped off his clothes, his eyes locked with hers. Slowly, as if he were savoring each torturing moment, he brought his lips to hers again. He unzipped her skirt, wriggling it over her hips, then removed her slip and stockings with incredible slowness, letting his fingers trail sensuously over her thighs. His lips followed the path his hands had made, lingering unbearably at sensitive hollows, making her moan and cry with uncontrollable desire.

"Ginny," he groaned, his voice catching in his throat. Just when she thought she could stand no more, he grasped her roughly and pulled her tightly against him. He kissed her deeply, his tongue probing her mouth as he joined his body to hers.

Gin felt as if she were in the midst of a hurricane, so powerful were the sensations whirling her into a vortex of pleasure. She gasped at the sweet agony he was putting her through, and Noah laughed huskily, caressing her with his hands and lips until she was quivering.

Just as Gin thought she would surely die from the torrent of ecstasy, they reached the zenith of the storm. Shudders racked her like a violent wind, abating ever so slowly to a calm, gentle breeze.

When she finally grew aware of her surroundings once again, Noah leaned over her, gently kissing her eyelids. He wrapped her in his arms, his hands softly caressing her back.

Gin snuggled against him, sighing with contentment. As incredible as it seemed, she knew she felt something very deep for this egotistical man, knew also that her feelings frightened her. She couldn't explain even to herself her conflicting emotions, but she agreed with Suzanne. There was a fine line between love and hate. Noah Grady had irritated her, persecuted her, chided her, and now he had made love to her. Strangely, she didn't feel guilty. Making love to him had felt as natural as being alive.

"Noah," Gin said later as she ran her fingers over his chest and arms, "all my beliefs have just been shattered."

"Mmm?" he mumbled lazily, kissing the tip of her

nose. "You'll regret that," he warned her when she
ran her fingers hesitantly down the thin line of hair
on his stomach. Noah inhaled sharply when her fingers
continued their downward motion. "What beliefs?"
he asked hoarsely.

"The gossips were wrong," she said, her expression
serious. "They only rate you a nine point eight."

Noah laughed, then grabbed her and held her beneath him, staring into her eyes. "You're not so bad
yourself, Ginny Selton. And you have the most beautiful blue eyes I've ever seen."

He kissed her lightly on the lips, then worked his
way slowly to her breasts. "Along with a voluptuous,
desirable body," he whispered.

Noah trailed his hands lower, and Gin responded
willingly. "I'll bet you say that to all the nurses," she
whispered back. She couldn't help but remember his
reputation and wondered if he cared for her as a person
as well as a desirable body.

"Just those who openly defy me." He grinned.
"Let's try that again," he continued. His voice was
husky and meaningful as he leaned toward her. "I
want to shatter the rest of your beliefs."

"Noah." Gin kissed him back, marveling at her
body's quick response. "We never did eat dinner."

chapter 6

GIN LEANED her head against Noah's shoulder, captivated by the monotonous sound of the windshield wipers sweeping snow off the car. She felt as if she were enclosed in a giant cocoon. The storm was raging around them, but the car was warm, and soft strains of classical music were coming from the radio, making the moment terribly romantic. Sighing contentedly, Gin snuggled closer to him.

"Tired?" Noah asked, smiling down at her. "We should be at your apartment in just a few minutes."

"No," Gin said, staring openly at his rugged features. Adonis reincarnated, Suzanne had described him that night so long ago. It was hard for Gin to believe that her feelings for Noah had changed so drastically in just a few short days. She still didn't think that what she felt for him was love, but whatever it was, she spent every waking moment—and some sleeping moments—thinking about him. She moved her head against the nubby texture of his jacket. It smelled faintly of tobacco mingled with the musky odor of his maleness. "Isn't it beautiful, Noah?" she asked, then grinned at her inability to communicate intelligently how she felt about the past few days. "The snow, I mean."

"More like treacherous." He kept his eyes fixed on the road. "Minnesota should have been deeded to the Eskimos long ago."

"This sounds odd, but I feel very secure despite the weather. Isn't that strange?"

"Ginny, your moods are beyond my comprehension." Although his words sounded clipped, he reached out a hand to gently caress her knee, and tiny shocks of pleasure made her feel weak. "Did you enjoy the musical?" he asked, then quickly removed his hand, catching the steering wheel as the car slid on the ice-packed street.

The spot where his hand had lain so lightly still tingled, and Gin hardly noticed that the car had swerved. She smiled in the darkness, grateful that he couldn't see her expression. She hadn't the vaguest idea what the musical had been about. Her entire awareness had been focused on Noah. She realized her attention span had been extremely limited the past few days and knew she had to pull herself together. Twenty-six-year-old women weren't supposed to act like starry-eyed teenagers!

"Have you fallen asleep on me?" Noah asked, moving his shoulder slightly without taking his attention off the slippery road.

Gin laughed lightly and started to speak but was interrupted by the high-pitched sound of his beeper. Noah groaned, then quickly pulled the car to the curb and flicked on the electronic contraption.

"Dr. Grady, call Lakeside Emergency Room, stat! Call Lakeside Emergency!" the voice commanded.

"I'll be right back," Noah told Gin, getting out of

the car and sprinting toward a public phone booth a few hundred feet away.

When he returned, his dark brows were drawn into a scowl. He shifted gears and turned sharply into the busy street. "Some kid totaled his car—and almost himself—on the Interstate," he snapped as he maneuvered into a lane of oncoming traffic. "I have to get there fast. Do you mind coming along?"

Gin knew she didn't really have a choice, but she appreciated that Noah had asked. She thought momentarily of the gossip that would follow their entrance into the emergency room, but the vision of a seriously injured patient overruled all the objections she might have otherwise made.

She clung to the upholstery as Noah careened through the slippery streets and wondered several times if *they* would arrive uninjured. But he handled the car expertly, and within moments they were pulling up at the arrival dock.

Noah grasped her hand as they raced together to the entrance, and she felt grateful at his slight squeeze of encouragement. His action seemed to tell her he was aware of her unspoken anxieties, and that he understood.

Once inside, Noah was abruptly swallowed up in a maze of confusion. Gin realized she wouldn't be allowed beyond the double doors, and she walked slowly toward the waiting area.

She felt distinctly out of place in her pale green dress and backless heels, and it dawned on her that this bustling, frenetic place was no longer her world. What was going on behind the formidable doors of the emergency room was no longer her concern.

Her discomfort only increased when she found a seat among the throng of people waiting their turn in the crowded emergency room. She picked up a col-

orful magazine and flipped through it absently, trying
to concentrate on page after page of swimsuits and
recipes, but her attention kept wandering to the sick
and injured people sitting patiently awaiting medical
attention.

In one corner of the room a middle-aged woman
was sobbing uncontrollably while a man held her in
his arms. Gin could see tears shining in his eyes too,
along with terror, but he held the woman with a stoic
expression, occasionally patting her on the back. Gin
knew instinctively that they were the parents of the
injured young man Noah was treating, and her heart
constricted with sympathy.

When she realized the curious eyes of the other
patients were also focused on the grieving couple, she
returned to her magazine, trying to force her mind to
absorb the printed words. Yet as each agonizing minute ticked by, she found herself glancing at them
again.

Although she felt like an intruder, she stared in
morbid fascination when they moved into the hallway.
The woman collapsed again in the man's arms when
a stretcher carrying her son was wheeled past. Moments later Noah swept through the door, issuing orders in a calm, assured manner.

"Keep his urine output up," she heard another voice
call after him. "He's a potential kidney donor."

When the father turned pale, Gin was struck by the
callousness of the remark. She watched Noah speak
briefly to the parents, then whirl away. They were
both crying openly now, the woman rambling hys-
terically about teenagers and cars.

How unfair life could be, Gin thought, acutely
aware of the cold efficiency of the system. Sickness,
impending death, and life-giving organs were every-
day occurrences in this sterile environment. Gin felt

an anguish for the couple that lurched in her stomach.

She threw the magazine aside and fled to the snack bar, unable to bear the bitter gall that closed her throat. She fumbled in her purse for some change then, grimacing, sipped the hot, rancid coffee she obtained from the vending machine.

Oh, how she regretted her helplessness! She desperately wanted to do something—anything—to help save the life of the boy that had lain so still on the stretcher. She clenched her fists at her side and willed herself to think about the musical she and Noah had attended. She mustn't dwell on her feelings of uselessness. There was nothing she could do, and even if she were still employed as a nurse, she would feel hopeless rage at her inability to be totally involved with her patient.

Sighing, she finished the coffee and headed back to the emergency room, avoiding the crowded waiting area.

"Excuse me," she said to a nurse at the desk. "When Dr. Grady returns, please tell him I'm waiting in the staff lounge."

A slim, dark-haired girl looked up from the papers on the desk. Her eyes took in Gin's clinging dress, and a knowing smile crept to her lips. "Well... welcome to the club," she said, her voice mocking. "It's always nice to meet your rival face to face."

Gin was a bit confused, but she had the distinct feeling the nurse had assessed her quickly, and that she was definitely the loser. "I-I wasn't aware I had a rival," she murmured.

"Yes, well, I am surprised he brought you here. He's usually a bit more discreet. I'm Catherine Timmits. I came after Mary Anne Harner... and before you, but I assure you I'll be seeing Noah again very soon."

"Oh," Gin said, as if the revelation and chrono-logical order were important. She knew she should just ignore the biting comments of the attractive nurse, but she couldn't command her body to move. She also knew that whatever she might say at this moment would only fuel the tongues of the gossips. She was very aware that the attention of every person in the corridor had been drawn to their conversation.

Catherine smiled vindictively at Gin's obvious dis-comfort. She tossed her hair over her shoulders and laughed softly. "It's a good thing Noah doesn't have a social disease, isn't it?" she said, then at Gin's shocked look, she pretended concern. "Oh, I'm sorry," she continued. "You didn't know. And you were probably thinking you were special."

"Since it's obvious that sharing Noah's bed is no guarantee of permanence," Gin finally managed to say, "perhaps we should compare caresses at a later date."

Gin turned on her heel, surprised that her thoughts were still coherent, and walked to the staff lounge, hoping she appeared nonchalant. She felt as if she'd been slapped in the face. Although she realized the nurse was being purposely spiteful, her attitude had been infuriating.

Gin was grateful for the semidarkness of the lounge. She tried to calm her shaking body while she thought about her scathing remark to Catherine Tim-mits. It had been unnecessary and now she regretted it—especially since it was echoing over and over in her mind.

Sharing Noah's bed is no guarantee of permanence, a voice kept screaming. I don't care, another part of her shouted back. Noah doesn't owe me anything! Certainly not a commitment. After all, they weren't in love. What she felt for Noah—well, it certainly wasn't love. She had *loved* Nick Carlin and look what had happened. You're lying, the voice nagged, if you don't love him why are you so upset?

Gin looked frantically around the room, searching for something to divert her thoughts. She almost wished she were reading the magazine again. Even bikini-clad models would have been preferable to the whirling confusion of her mind.

She stared at the notices cluttering a bulletin board and forced herself to read a typewritten sign. "Straight Woman To Share with Same, Large, Roomy Apartment near Hospital." A notice in the next row advertised a local pizzeria, and another sign said, "Experience Caring. American College of Midwifery."

"In-service Education," read another. "Presented by Noah Grady, M.D." There were several other notices, but Gin realized as she stared at the paper printed with Noah's name that even something as mundane as a bulletin board brought her painful encounters with him to mind.

Noah Grady and Nick Carlin were so much alike they could have been clones, she thought. They were both arrogant, handsome, and capriciously mendacious men who collected women like some people collected stamps.

She turned away and picked up a medical magazine. She flipped through it, her thoughts centered on the agony she had felt when she found Nick Carlin in the arms of another woman. Now, just when she thought she could forget, Noah's indiscretions had brought her full circle.

Gin had resumed her pacing when she finally heard Noah's voice in the corridor. She went to the door to meet him, irritated that, despite her conclusions, she had sat patiently waiting for him while hour after hour had ticked by. She was totally exhausted from her

unwelcome musings, and unreasonably furious with
him.

Gin stopped abruptly at the entrance when she
heard Catherine's voice, too. As Noah approached the
desk, she watched calmly, almost detached, aware
that he hadn't noticed her.

"Dr. Grady," Catherine Timmits said to him with
a sultry smile, "you forgot to sign the chart." She
glanced at Gin, flashed her a malicious look, and
placed her hand possessively on Noah's arm, man-
aging to maneuver him so that all Gin could see were
their gestures.

Noah bent his head when Catherine spoke, leaning
close to her, then rested his hand on her shoulder. He
nodded, scrawled his signature across the papers she
handed him, and gave a short halflaugh.

"No problem," he said in his lazy, seductive voice.
"I'll pick you up at seven o'clock Thursday. Be ready
on time for a change."

All the hurt and anger Gin had repressed bubbled
to the surface as the hateful image of Nick's unfaithful
act flashed before her mind's eye. She saw so vividly
the naked, intertwined limbs, the passionate embrace
that it could have been happening now. She closed her
eyes and leaned against the doorway for support, fighting the nausea that roiled in her stomach.

When she opened her eyes again, Catherine was
staring triumphantly at her. Her look conveyed to Gin
that although she may have won the verbal battle hours
ago, Catherine would win the war.

Noah turned, an expression that Gin couldn't de-
cipher crossing his handsome features, then flashed
an indolent grin at her. "There you are," he said.
"Ready to go home?"

Aware that Catherine was watching her, Gin gave

him a halting smile and walked toward him as if she hadn't just overheard his conversation. She marveled at his guiltless attitude. Compared to Nick, Noah was the champion of deceit.

"How's the boy?" she murmured, noticing the lines of fatigue on his face.

"Not good." Noah sighed, running a hand through his hair, the familiar gesture making Gin's heart contract with pain. "The vultures are waiting for him to die, but I'll be damned if they get his kidneys before I've done everything possible."

Gin nodded, and they left the building in silence. Although the icy conditions had worsened, Gin remembered very little of the ride back to her apartment. Noah had to concentrate completely on the road, and she knew he was also very upset about the condition of his patient. She leaned her head back on the seat, carefully emptying her mind of all thought. She started with surprise when in what seemed only minutes, they pulled into the underground garage of her apartment.

Trancelike, she walked beside Noah to her door and politely handed him the keys. He looked at her with a puzzling expression, then opened the apartment, standing aside while she entered. Gin flipped on a light and sighed, throwing her purse onto a nearby chair. She waved her hand toward a small portable bar. "Want a drink? Or some coffee?"

Noah shook his head, tossing her keys on the chair beside her purse. "Is the prospect of gossip about us that upsetting?" he asked.

"No," she admitted truthfully.

"Something's bothering you, Ginny. What is it?"

"I'm tired," she hedged. "I'd just like to go to bed."

"That's exactly what I had in mind," he said softly.

A devilish smile lit up his weary face.

"I have a headache, Grady," she said, turning away from his probing gaze.

Noah moved behind her and placed his hands at either side of her head. His fingers felt cool and soothing at her temples. "That's a convenient cliché," he whispered into her ear, his voice low and husky. "Let me massage it away."

"No, please don't," Gin said more sharply than she intended, moving away from his hands. The hot surge of desire in her thighs at his touch disgusted her. "It's nothing, Grady," she snapped.

"I can always tell when you're angry at me," he said, his voice sending shivers up her spine in spite of her anger. "You call me Grady."

"I'm not angry at you," she insisted, furious at her treacherous body. "I'm very tired, and tomorrow is my first day at my new job. If you don't mind, I'd like to get some rest."

Noah arched an eyebrow at her. "This probably isn't a good time, considering your mood, but I've been meaning to talk to you about that. I may as well get it over with."

From a pocket in his suit jacket he pulled out a small package that was wrapped exactly like the one he'd given her on Christmas Day.

"Another flashlight?" she asked wryly as he shoved the box into her hands. "Your imagination astounds me."

"Yes, well, I thought we might have that conversation again. I really blew it the other night when I first gave this to you. I can't say I'm sorry about how the evening ended, but I meant to say that I think you belong in nursing."

Gin flushed at his reminder of the passionate night they had shared and silently cursed her abandoned response to him. How could she have been so foolish as to have gotten involved with him? She turned away from his intense gaze. "I don't see why my choice of a career continues to be any of your concern," she said, her sour voice matching her mood.

"Because I've made it my concern," he retorted. "You're too qualified to work in a grocery store. If you won't go back to the hospital, why don't you become a school nurse or an industrial nurse?" he suggested.

"Or a private-duty nurse? Or a surgical nurse? Or a pediatric nurse?" she mimicked. "Because I made a decision and I intend to stick to it. Because I can't stand being evasive to patients. Because I'm tired of walking that narrow line between knowledge and practice. And because none of those are my specialty!" Gin's voice had risen throughout her tirade, and her last sentence was an angry staccato.

Noah caught her hand in his and swung her around until she was facing him. "Then maybe you'll appreciate my proposition," he said. "I'll be needing a nurse soon. I finish my residency in a couple of months, and since neuro is your specialty, you can work for me. I can offer you an excellent package." He grinned, then continued. "A good salary, attractive hours, and a pleasant employer."

"Does your package include being my lover?" The sarcastic comment seemed to escape her lips without volition, and, although Gin immediately regretted it, she couldn't retract it.

"That would be one of the fringe benefits." Noah stared intently at her, his gray eyes darkening with undisguised desire. "One you enjoyed previously," he added.

"No contracts or commitments?" Gin tried to sound casual, but she was fully aware that her offhand question was charged with a double meaning.

Something seemed to flash in the depths of Noah's eyes as he looked at her, but it was gone before Gin could define it. "Just a mutually beneficial agreement," he said after a moment. "And good references if it doesn't work out for either of us."

The anxiety that had started in the pit of her stomach when she first posed the question became a raging pain. Gin jerked her hand away from his and turned around so he couldn't see how his words had devastated her. "Thank you, *Noah,*" she said, "but I have no intentions of becoming your nurse...or your lover. I-I made a mistake the other night. I realize now I was...lonely and vulnerable. Now if you'll please leave, I'd like to get some sleep."

"Damn it, Ginny!" Noah grasped her arm and pulled her roughly against him. "I know when you're lying to me!"

Her heart pounding, Gin twisted away from his grip. If she allowed him to make love to her again, she knew she would be totally lost. Aware that he could easily subdue her with his strength and overwhelm her with the wild force of her own passion, she lashed out at him. "Grady!" she shouted. "You may think in your conceited, smug mind that you know me, but you haven't the vaguest idea what you're talking about." Gin prayed he couldn't detect the ring of falsehood in her voice. "If you make love to me now, it will be rape. I'm sure there are many women who would be willing to endure your caresses. I'm not one of them!"

Noah's eyes flashed with anger. "Ginny, I've had a long, frustrating night. Your shallow and distrustful attitude doesn't help." He sighed deeply. "I'd like some comfort and understanding for a change."

"Then go bother Mary Anne Harner or Catherine Timmits!"

Sudden realization dawned in his eyes. "You're jealous," he said. "What did Catherine say to you tonight?"

"Nothing! And I am not jealous! I just don't intend to contribute to your notorious reputation. God, Grady, there are so many women in your life we could hold a convention and elect officers. 'The Former Lovers of Noah Grady would like to welcome you to its first weekly meeting. On our agenda tonight is his latest flame speaking to you about—"

Noah grasped her arms and shook her slightly, although Gin was very aware of the effort he was exerting to maintain control of his temper. "What the hell have *I* done?" he demanded. "Ginny, you've got your parents' deaths and your fiancé's betrayal so mixed up in your mind that you're blaming yourself for both and now punishing me for what happened to you six months ago."

"You don't know what you're talking about!" Gin snapped.

"You're in love with me, aren't you, Ginny?"

"No!" she cried, frantically searching her mind for a way to deny it. How had he guessed so soon? But she was too proud to admit his words were true. "You'd like that, wouldn't you, Grady?" she told him. "Another conquest falling at your feet. Well I could never love you! Your brilliance amazes me, Grady. You can't even understand simple facts. I love Nick Carlin!"

She sensed his instant withdrawal. His face became flushed with fury. Immediately she regretted the lie. She loved Noah, not Nick. But she must never let him know that. He would never love her back the way she loved him.

"You're irrational, Ginny." Noah's voice was so cold it could have been chipped from ice. "I thought we were two mature adults who could enjoy a relationship without getting hung up about it, but I was obviously wrong. I think I'll confirm your jealous accusations and give Mary Anne or Catherine a visit."

He turned away, grabbing his coat and reaching the door in a few swift steps. He slammed it shut behind him. The impact caused a crystal figurine to topple from a nearby end table and crash to the floor in a thousand shards.

Gin collapsed on the sofa, allowing the tears she had held in check to flow freely down her cheeks. Noah was gone, and she had sent him away. It was best this way. Noah was only interested in a sexual companion. How had he put it? A mutually beneficial agreement. But she found cold comfort in realizing she'd done the right thing.

Suddenly angry all over again, Gin sat up and dried her tears, picturing Noah and Catherine locked in an embrace. Well, she was not about to let Noah Grady destroy her! Tomorrow she would start a new job, and along with it she would begin a new life.

She swept up the tiny pieces of glass and grabbed Noah's unopened present, dumping them all into the trash. She would put Noah Grady and the entire world of medicine where they belonged! Gin knew she was indulging in a childish tantrum, but nevertheless her actions gave her a perverse satisfaction.

chapter 7

"I MADE A vow last night to never see you again."
Gin held the door ajar, giving Noah her most con-
temptuous look.

"Well, unvow it!" he told her, pushing the door
open. "Unless you believe in apparitions, I'm here
and you're seeing me."

"This is growing wearisome," she snapped back.
As he strode arrogantly into the room, it struck her
that, considering the ease with which he entered her
apartment, he might as well have had his own key.

"You're damned right!" he said. "I can't for the
life of me figure out why I keep returning for your
abuse."

"My abuse!" she cried. "Even Don Juan had a
sense of honor! What happened to Mary Anne and
Catherine?"

"They're fine." He flashed her a malevolent grin.

"Would you like a detailed elaboration?"

"That really won't be necessary," she commented dryly. "Tell me Noah," she said, being very careful to use his first name, "why do you keep bothering me?"

"The hell if I know," he answered. "Maybe I just want to add another notch to my belt." He strode over to where she kept a small number of liquor bottles and poured himself a tumbler of whiskey. Except for a glass of wine now and then, this was the first time Gin had seen him take a drink.

"Actually," he continued, looking at her over the rim of the amber-tinged glass, "I pride myself on being able to manage difficult cases. Perhaps you're a challenge."

"And after the cure is effected, the patient is forgotten in the thrill of another difficult case," Gin added for him.

"You have an irritating habit of masking cowardice with indignation, Ginny." He stared at her for a long moment, then slugged down the drink and poured another. "I'm tired of playing silly teenage games with you. 'He loves me, he loves me not' is for children. Mature relationships are based on trust."

"You don't know the meaning of the word, Grady," she snapped back.

"I may not have been a very trustworthy person where women are concerned for most of my life, but at least I don't delude myself or other people by indulging in infantile contrivances or hysterical denials." He went back to the bar and refilled his glass a third time. "Mr. Murphy was readmitted today," he added when he had turned back to her. "Which is the real reason I came here tonight. He said to say hello. He heard through the grapevine that I have access to his favorite nurse. However pleasant or unpleasant that association is, I neglected to mention."

"How is he?" Gin asked, concerned.

"Sick."

"No kidding, Noah. Has his brain tumor spread already?"

"Yes, plus it's the effects of the radiation." Noah sat down in a chair, leaning his head back wearily and closing his eyes.

"I'm sorry." Gin wanted to reach out and smooth the worry from his furrowed brow, but she clenched her hands in front of her instead. If she touched him, she'd be lost.

"Sorry?" He laughed harshly and sipped his drink. "That's a fitting epitaph for his tombstone. Look, Ginny," he said sharply, "I don't like cancer protocol any more than you do, but I swore an oath years ago to do everything in my power to conserve life."

"Noah, I didn't say anything about your choice of treatment." Gin poured a glass of cola and sat down on the sofa across from him. Apparently this conversation was just beginning.

"You didn't have to." Noah rose from the chair and paced restlessly back and forth across the thick rug. "It's all right there—in the way you look at me. He was supposed to have six months more," he spat, disgusted. Noah looked as if his world had fallen apart and he didn't quite know how to put it back together again.

"But he doesn't," Gin said softly. She ached to comfort him but didn't dare. "That's not your fault, Noah."

"Sometimes I wonder," he said at last. "The mortality rate in neurosurgery is phenomenal, Ginny." He stared morosely into the amber liquid of his drink, a scowl marring his features. "You learn to detach your emotions in this profession—you have to in order to survive." He looked up at her, and his expression suddenly lightened. Placing his drink on an end table, he grabbed her hands, and pulled her up from the sofa. "Let's go on a sleigh ride," he urged her with boyish enthusiasm. "It's a beautiful night."

Stunned by his abrupt change of mood and suppressing a wild urge to kiss his sensitive mouth, Gin jerked her hands away from his. "Was all that talk just a ploy to make me complacent and sympathetic?" she demanded to know.

"Is that what you really think?" he asked, looking warmly into her eyes. "I know I'm egotistical and aggressive and many other things that aren't terribly desirable in a man, and I'm aware that my detachment spills over into my personal life, but I'm asking you to share an evening with me. Is there anything wrong with that?"

"I think it's a little late in our relationship for sleigh rides, Noah. What happened between us last night is still very vivid to me."

"And to me. My first failure. It's difficult to admit to failing, you know." He paused a moment, looking down at her. "I'm sorry I'm not a knight in shining armor, Ginny, but *I* stopped believing in fairy tales long ago. Let's just enjoy tonight."

Gin looked up at his handsome face, at the gray eyes that could be so steely at times. She wanted to say so much, but would doing so open all the old wounds? Noah was a complicated man, and so unreachable at times that he frightened her.

"I hope you have warm snuggies," he said when she didn't answer, grabbing her hand and dragging her toward the bedroom. "Otherwise I'll have to loan you a pair of mine."

He yanked a pair of brown slacks, a beige and yellow turtleneck sweater, and a pair of brown sheepskin-lined boots from her closet while Gin stared at him, perplexed.

He piled the clothes on her bed with a sly grin on his face, then rifled through her drawers, pulling out heavy socks and thermal underwear. Hesitating only a moment, and with a brief arch of his eyebrow when he found them, he added a chocolate-brown bra and panties that were trimmed with rows of delicate, sheer beige lace.

Stealing a surreptitious glance at her, he selected a bottle of expensive French perfume from the array of cosmetics on her dresser and inhaled deeply of the flowery aroma. Gin watched, holding her breath as he walked toward her.

He reached out to remove the pins from her hair, giving a seductive half laugh when it tumbled about her shoulders and down her back in a cascade of golden curls. He twined his fingers in its soft mass and pulled her toward him. "Shall I help you dress?" he asked before his lips met hers.

Gin felt herself quiver in response to the raw passion in his ragged voice, and when his lips finally claimed hers, she reached up her arms to encircle his neck, the now familiar sensation his embrace evoked pounding with a wild intensity through her pliant body.

With a groan he pressed her against his length, and she reveled in his hard need, in the driving fervor of his kiss, and in the overpowering emotion coursing through her.

Her breath quickened when Noah's lips moved to the tiny pulse in the curve of her throat. His hands moved to unbotton her dress, then slipped it from her shoulders. She shuddered when the cool air touched her heated flesh. He unhooked her bra, and his hands caressed every intimate hollow, exploring the bare, swelling peaks of her breasts, then moving up to sensuously tantalize her shoulders, then dipping lower to gently caress the silken softness of her hips.

"Ginny," he whispered, his voice thick with emotion. "Oh God, I want you." His lips trailed fire down her throat until at last they reached the full rise of her breast and lingered, teasing, torturing, until she moaned with pleasure.

He led her to the bed, and his mouth ravished hers again. She stretched against him, savoring the feel of him, the taste of him, aching with overwhelming need. The ardent embrace left her insensitive to anything but their mutual need, and she succumbed to the violent force of their arousal, soaring into oblivion.

After they had reached the tumult of their passion, Noah enfolded her in his arms and, lifting her heavy hair, kissed the dampness at the nape of her neck. Gin stretched and snuggled against his chest, sighing with pleasure at the languor that seemed to possess her.

Noah laughed, a light teasing chuckle, and to her surprise, slapped her playfully on one bare hip. "Get up, lazybones," he said. "The frozen North awaits you, or have you already forgotten our sleigh ride?"

Gin groaned and snuggled closer to him. "Noah, it's cold out there," she mumbled.

"Right," he agreed, reaching for the thermal underwear he had piled on the bed and handing it to her. "Would you prefer going as you are?"

Gin looked up at him and laughed. "I would *prefer* a warm beach, Noah," she teased, then grabbed her clothes from his hands. "But since you insist, I'll settle for a sleigh ride."

The moonlight traced a path of hundreds of tiny diamonds on the new-fallen snow, and above her Gin recognized several constellations in the star-studded sky. She snuggled closer to Noah under the down-filled comforter, enjoying the way the wind ruffled her long hair and teased her already pinked cheeks.

The gay tinkle of the sleigh bells attached to two huge, brown-dappled horses pulling the cutter echoed in the silent night. On either side of the trail giant, stately trees shot up into the sky, their bare limbs snow-capped and luminous. Tiny icicles, catching the light from the moon, reflected from dark spruces interspersed among the trees.

"Oh, this is so beautiful," Gin breathed, wondering if any other moment could ever match the spectacular phenomenon of this wintry night.

"Aren't you glad you came?" Noah whispered into her ear, his breath making the tiny hairs on her neck stand on end.

"As I recall, I didn't have a choice," she whispered back, delicious shivers running through her body. "I would have been quite content in my warm bedroom."

She thought of the irrevocable choice she had made in that room a few hours ago. She loved Noah hopelessly. She had acknowledged it last night, when they had fought so bitterly, and had accepted it in that tense moment in her apartment when Noah had looked so devastated by Mr. Murphy's condition. When he had kissed her, she had decided that she wanted him, that she would risk being hurt again, even though her decision was based on emotion rather than intellect.

Would Noah ever be able to settle down with just one woman? She kept wondering. He hadn't exactly admitted he'd spent the night with another woman; he had only intimated it. Given the opportunity, she was certain she could convince him that other women in his life would be extraneous baggage. Besides, the hungry, forceful way he had possessed her body a short while ago had given her hope that he wanted her—and only her.

Gin reached for his hand under the warm blankets, reassured by the instant response of his fingers as they made tantalizing swirls in her palm.

"The best thing about living in this vast, frozen wasteland is undressing a beautiful woman," he whispered into her ear. "Underneath all those layers of clothing is a soft, warm, passionate body." He slipped his hands under her jacket, seeking and finding the bare skin beneath her sweater.

His light touch set every nerve in her body on fire. He laughed huskily at her low moan, then kissed her throat, eventually claiming her lips with exquisite torture.

Gin was lost in the eternity of his embrace, hungrily returning his kiss. She gasped when he moved his lips again to her neck. As if from afar, she heard the crackle of snow as the runners broke crusted ice, and when she opened her eyes, the stars seemed to be swirling in the night sky. She moaned again, ready to yield to her throbbing desire, but the shouted orders of the driver to the horses brought her back to reality.

She flushed with embarrassment when she realized the driver had more than likely overheard her passionate moans.

"Noah, the driver," she hissed, pointing to the ram-rod straight back of the man steering the lumbering sled.

"You prefer him?" Noah asked with a grin, moving his hand around her back to unhook her lacy bra. "I get it, you like the outdoor type." He drew his fingers in agonizing slowness around to her chest, finally cupping a breast in his hand. His thumb flicked the taut nipple tenderly, and his lips met hers again in a warm, probing kiss.

"Noah, you're impossible!" Gin laughed lightly and wriggled away from his touch. "Wait until we get home," she whispered. "I'll show you what I like."

"I hope it's lecherous, sex-starved neurosurgeons." He stared into her eyes, his own filled with promise, then, when Gin yawned in his face, he laughed throwing his head back and shaking with mirth.

"I'm sorry." She laughed too, quickly covering her mouth with her hand. "I'm afraid your ravenous appetite will have to be assuaged another time, Noah Grady, for now that I'm a working girl again, I seem to be exhausted."

"I'm not averse to spending the night." His eyes shone with boyish amusement.

"Oh, but I am," Gin said, at once serious. "Don't try to push my good humor too far, Dr. Grady."

"If you're not careful, Ginny Selton, I'll push *you* into the cold, wet snow and make mad, passionate love to you until you beg me to spend the night."

"Promises, promises." Gin grinned at his threat and yawned again. "Noah, I can't believe I'm so tired. It must be this fresh air."

"I prefer to think you're sated, Ginny," he said, reminding her again of their wild, abandoned session in her bed only hours ago. "But in the future I'll have to remember that you prefer indoor sports."

Gin's heart hammered in her chest at his casual mention of their future. She prayed she wouldn't regret her impetuous decision to risk everything to win his love. She snuggled against him, willing herself to forget the complications of her life just for tonight.

The next day Noah had managed to arrange a morning off and, although Gin knew it was irresponsible of her, she called in sick. She dressed hurriedly after his phone call, pulling on a full skirt in hues of beige and gold and a matching bulky knit sweater in deep rust. She drew a brush through her long hair, fluffing it around her face the way Noah liked it, then dabbed blusher on her cheeks, finishing off with pale lip gloss.

She gave her hair a final, satisfied pat in the mirror just as Noah rang the buzzer. Grabbing her only real luxury, a fox fur jacket her parents had given her several years ago, she met him at the door with a wide smile. "I told you I could be ready in fifteen minutes."

Noah smiled down at her. "You've managed to amaze me once again," he said. "But this is a shopping expedition, not a fashion show."

"Thanks for the compliment, if I may take it that way. I gather you like my taste." She twirled, showing off the soft leather boots that hugged her slim calves. "Half price at my local shoe store. I'm lucky I have such large feet."

He watched her with one hand on the doorjamb. "Ginny," he said when she stopped before him, breathless, "I think I'd like anything you put on, but there's one thing in particular I like very much on you, and that's nothing at all."

Gin's face flamed, as it always did when he mentioned his physical attraction to her. "Sometimes you're imperious, Noah," she stammered, trying to cover her embarrassment.

"And you are a puzzle," he countered. "Women have always been a mystery to me. You'd think that after living with five sisters I'd have developed some understanding of feminine temperament, but I seem to have failed miserably. What did I say now to upset you?"

Gin laughed at his contrite expression. "Here I thought you were the expert on women. I believe you intimated as much just a few days ago."

He laughed, too. "Living with my reputation isn't easy, Ginny. I have to bluff a lot. It's very tiresome, but it's become an ingrained part of my fantastic personality."

Gin shook her head in mock anger. "Such problems, and your humility is touching. Don't we have a lot of shopping to do? We'll never get it done standing in my hallway."

They spent most of the day wandering into and out of department stores in a giant enclosed shopping mall. Noah seemed to be at a loss about what to send his sisters and their children for belated Christmas gifts. He knew nothing about his nieces' and nephews' ages, and still less about their tastes, and he took Gin's suggestions gladly, almost hastily.

By early afternoon the overpowering heat of the stores combined with Gin's heavy sweater and coat and the hordes of shoppers searching for bargains had taken its toll on her. Gin was hot and tired, and her feet felt like two fiery pokers inside the new boots, which had begun to chafe her heels.

In contrast Noah looked cool and comfortable in his slacks and tweed jacket. He strode beside her, his hand resting on the small of her back, content to dodge the crowds while they piled package after package into a giant shopping bag that he carried effortlessly.

Laughing as they wove their way out of their tenth toy store, Noah wiped the perspiration away from her temples. "I thought you preferred indoor sports," he teased.

"This isn't a sport, Noah, it's brutal torture, and I think I'm going to drop dead any moment now."

He steered her toward a snack bar. "Let's stop for a snack before you collapse and I have to give you mouth-to-mouth resuscitation like a dedicated doctor."

"Why didn't you think to mail your family's gifts before the holidays, Noah?" Gin asked when they were seated in a booth.

Noah settled the purchases beside him. "I wouldn't have had your expert assistance then," he said and laughed. "Truthfully, I didn't collect my monthly stipend from Lakeside until today. You seem to think I'm teasing when I tell you how poor senior residents are."

"Did you pay for your education?" Gin asked, gratefully sipping the cola the waitress brought. Her mouth was so dry and parched she could have been hiking in the desert the past few hours.

Noah nodded, taking a sip of his coffee. "My father complained all his life about having to marry off five daughters. They helped all they could, but weddings seem to cost a lot these days, especially Italian ones." He shrugged his shoulders, then smiled again. "How about helping me pick out my Mercedes next month? I have a hot date with a car dealer who's willing to give me all the credit I want, and I think I like your sensible judgment."

Gin lifted her eyebrows in surprise. "An expensive car doesn't sound like you," she said. "I thought you were a dedicated doctor who was willing to sacrifice his life for the good of his patients."

"And my sudden interest in material possessions makes you think I'm greedy? I'm sorry, Ginny, but I don't see anything wrong in wanting to fulfill a few dreams. I've worked hard these past ten years, and I've made a lot of sacrifices. My private practice means a great deal to me. I plan to work with determination to make it succeed, and I don't intend to begrudge myself the rewards."

"I see," Gin said.

"So now my armor is tarnished in your eyes." Noah motioned to the sandwiches the waitress set down before them. "Shall we declare peace until we've eaten?"

Gin laughed and took a bite of her chicken salad

sandwich, then noticed a small child in the next booth. She judged him to be about two years old. He was blond and had huge brown eyes that were heavily fringed with the longest lashes she had ever seen.

Gin admired the intense concentration on his face as he tried to reach the tall glass made even taller by the addition of a straw he had proudly thrust into it. His mother was arranging her purchases and didn't realize he was having difficulty until the glass spilled on the table. She scolded him, slapping his hands, and mopped up the syrupy liquid with a napkin. Gin watched a hurt, confused expression cross his cherubic face. When his lower lip quivered dangerously, she smiled. "Do you like children, Noah?" she said before she realized she had verbalized her thoughts. Her face flamed, but she covered her discomfort by bending over her sandwich. What a time for wishful thinking!

Noah looked up from his own sandwich and threw a glance over his shoulder at the child, who was now bawling boisterously. "I never really thought much about it, Ginny. I haven't had time to consider home and hearth, and fatherhood hasn't been one of my goals. In fact, I've tried very hard to avoid that particular trap." He grinned, continuing to watch the child's antics and the mother's acute embarrassment. "That little guy is a real heart-tugger, however."

Gin wanted to pursue his comment about avoiding fatherhood but didn't quite know how to tell him she didn't need continuous reminders of his past reputation, particularly from him. She was saved from the uncomfortable discussion by the child's mother, who muttered something to them about shopping with children as she left the snack bar with her little boy.

Noah looked down at Gin's untouched plate. "No wonder you're thin," he said. "You don't eat."

"And I can't understand why you're not overweight," she countered, willing herself to keep silent about his previous comment. Perhaps he hadn't intended it to sound quite the way she had taken it.

Noah laughed and patted his stomach. "I can hardly wait for another meal from your kitchen. You make some mean sweet potatoes, Ginny Selton," he said, reminding her of the Christmas dinner they had shared after making love all afternoon. "How about tomorrow night?"

"Why not tonight?" she suggested. "Burning food is my culinary specialty, or do you have another date?"

He didn't seem to notice her final question. Instead of an immediate answer, he scowled. "I have to get back to the hospital," he said finally. "I feel guilty about today. I left Dr. Michaels in charge, and I'm worried about Jim Brandner. Besides," he added, tracing her jaw with his fingertip, "you've served your usefulness already. I have to get these presents in the mail before it's someone's birthday."

"So that's all a woman is to you," Gin teased back. "Useful."

"I can't think of any other purpose." Noah scrunched up his eyebrows as if deep in thought. "Unless it's to warm my bed at night."

"You're lucky I don't unleash my feminist beliefs on you, Noah Grady. But for some reason I seem to be too tired."

"You're just afraid to tangle with me, Ginny. You always lose. But I'd love to have dinner with you tomorrow night."

Gin was becoming somewhat irritated, in spite of levity of their banter. Noah's attitude toward women seemed to reflect his overbearing personality, and she wondered if he didn't really believe his own utterings. As they left the restaurant she realized that their relationship—if that was the correct term for their stormy moments together—was a continuous challenge to her.

chapter 8

THE NEXT DAY Gin was practically useless at work. Thursdays were typically busy days. As she rang up thousands of items brought to her counter by throngs of housewives the hours flashed by, but she couldn't seem to do anything right. She jammed the register and forgot how to change the tape, fiddling with it uselessly as a long line formed at her register. Her lack of concentration was particularly evident that afternoon when a seemingly sweet little old man made a scene because she didn't bag his jar of jelly upside down. It had broken, spilling a sticky mass over the bag and soiling the man's denture cleanser. His loudly voiced complaint, which everyone in the store heard, made her feel incredibly incompetent.

Ignoring the service manager's scowl, Gin punched out as soon as she could and rushed to the shopping mall. She still had to pick up the ingredients for dinner, but first she wanted to purchase the sexy, deep coral lounging gown she had noticed on sale yesterday. She shouldn't spend more money on loungewear, she knew, but it was such a good deal she couldn't resist. She had fallen in love with it, but had been too embarrassed to buy it with Noah present. She wanted to surprise him by wearing it tonight.

Gin bought the gown, then rushed back and picked up the things she would need for their meal, throwing them indiscriminately into a cart. Once back at her apartment, she chilled the salad and blended sauce for Cherries Jubilee. She unwrapped the steaks and placed them on the counter, pleased that she still had time for a leisurely bath.

Pouring liberal amounts of the French perfume Noah liked into the water, Gin relaxed and let the fragrant bath soothe her. Finally she slipped into the gown after she had vigorously toweled her body dry. She checked her reflection in the mirror. The gown was perfect, sexy and flattering without being overtly seductive. Dabbing some lip gloss in a matching color on her mouth, she rushed into the kitchen to finish dinner.

Gin moved about the room, humming a popular tune while she placed freshly laundered linen napkins, her best china and silver, and two slender candles on the table. She checked the time. Noah was late. What could have happened to him? When she realized she was behaving like a child who had been offered a forbidden treat and couldn't wait for it, she laughed and settled in a nearby chair with a novel.

Another hour passed. Gin gave up on the novel and wandered restlessly from room to room, flipping the television set on and off and picking up magazine after magazine, only to discard them all unread. She watched the leaves of romaine in the Caesar salad wilt as hour after hour ticked by, and still he didn't call or arrive.

As Gin was putting the thick sirloin steaks back into the refrigerator, she realized where Noah must be. A sharp pain swept over her, and she leaned against the cool, hard metal of the door, trembling with anguish. Thursday at seven, he had told Catherine Timmits. Oh, God! she moaned. Why had she trusted him? Why had she let herself care! She shook her head back and forth in denial, and a fierce, cold rage grasped her, stilling the trembling and leaving her mind a blur.

She undressed with incredible slowness, recalling every caress they had shared in the past as she stared into her dresser mirror, thinking of how Nick and now Noah had betrayed her. Why was she constantly attracted to Janus-faced men? Bitter experience hadn't taught her much! She should have realized long ago that men—at least the ones she was unfortunate enough to fall in love with—indulged their sexual appetites wherever they pleased!

She slept fitfully, refusing to succumb to tears. Noah wasn't worth crying over, she decided, but she knew in her heart that she wouldn't be able to resist his charming manner the moment he returned to her arms. Yet her seeming willingness to destroy her life by falling in love with unfaithful men must end!

Gin sat staring at greasy french fries and a soggy hamburger. Her stomach churned with revulsion. The combination of disgusting food and probing stares from hospital personnel was almost more than she could tolerate. She looked up at the clock again. She'd been sitting in The Nook for fifteen miserable minutes, and still Noah hadn't arrived.

Perhaps if she sat patiently for another few moments she would have a convenient excuse to escape from this travesty of a restaurant, as well as what she expected to be a very difficult encounter with him.

When he had called early that morning, insisting she meet him on her lunch hour, Gin had almost refused. The very sound of his voice had infuriated her, but she was anxious to know exactly how deep he would bury himself as he attempted to hide his unfaithfulness.

He hadn't bothered to explain his absence last night, telling her he had to be in surgery in five minutes and he'd tell her over lunch about how unbelievably busy the previous day had been.

Gin sighed and looked up from her unappetizing meal to see Noah at the door. She watched him stride across the room to her, his masculinity apparent in every step, and her heart constricted with pain. She loved him so much it hurt!

Noah took in her orange and brown polyester uniform with a cursory glance, then grinned in that very special way of his. "Well, if it isn't the food mogul. Have they moved you up to checker yet, or are you still bagging?"

"In addition to bagging, I started checking a couple days ago," Gin snapped. "I've told you before that my career problems are none of your business."

"My, my," he chided. "You're in a good humor today. Have you finally realized that a grocery store is not where you belong? Quit, Ginny. My offer still stands." He reached into his shirt pocket and handed her his pocket flashlight. "Or are you still running away from your problems?"

"The world should be grateful you chose neurosurgery instead of psychiatry, Noah. I can hardly wait to hear your Freudian theories." Gin picked up the flashlight and rolled it in her hand. "What do you suggest I do for the next six weeks to support myself while you finish your residency? No reputable employer would hire me for that length of time." She placed the flashlight on the table between them, aware of the significance of her gesture.

He picked the flashlight back up and pocketed it. "Then you finally admit I'm right. You belong back in nursing."

"Yes. I admit that *some* of your assumptions are right, and I'm thinking about your offer," she said. She nearly blurted out: I'm thinking about more than your offer. I'm thinking about what an untrustworthy person you are and how much I love you anyway. "But you didn't answer my question," she continued out loud. "What am I to do in the meantime?"

Noah reached across the table and took her hand in his. "There's this pleasant arrangement called roommates."

"Straight woman to share with same?" Gin shook her head. "I'm afraid that's not for me. I can't stand someone else's panty hose hanging in my bathroom."

"I was referring to someone who doesn't wear panty hose." He twirled his finger in her palm. "Namely me."

Gin jerked her hand from his, remembering his still unexplained absence of the previous evening. "That might cramp your style, Noah," she said, biting her tongue to keep from blurting out her accusations.

"It would be worth it just to be able to cut my expenses in half. I shouldn't have to remind you again that residents are poor, especially when they're trying to save every penny to open an office and buy a car." As if on impulse he stood halfway up and leaned across the table, kissing her full on the lips. "I forgot to say hello."

Gin looked nervously around the busy restaurant, flushing deeply. "I find it really difficult to follow your conversation sometimes, Noah, the way you skip around." She had wanted to say she had a difficult time understanding why he *played* around, but thought better of it. The Nook, filled to capacity with curious nurses and doctors, wasn't the place for the screaming match that would ensue if she pursued her suspicions.

They fell silent when the waitress brought Noah's food and refilled Gin's coffee cup. Glancing at his watch, he began to wolf down his hamburger as if he were starving. Gin stared in horrified fascination as he ate with relish. He hadn't even noticed the grease dripping from his burger.

"Didn't they teach you in medical school what this kind of food could do to your body?"

He stopped in mid-bite and looked at her untouched plate. "Eat up," he ordered, munching on a french fry that might have been dipped in a bottle of vegetable oil. "It's not as bad as the hospital cafeteria."

Gin made a strangling sound but picked up her sandwich and took several small, reluctant bites, thinking that at any moment her stomach might reject it right there on the table.

"Eat!" Noah commanded each time she paused, stealing her french fries as he spoke.

When they had finished, Gin looked up from her plate at her companion. "Noah, every time we eat together you badger me into licking my plate clean like an obedient dog." Then it dawned on her that she had almost forgotten to be angry at him.

Noah picked up the sprig of parsley lying on her plate. "Not quite clean, Ginny. Open up."

"That's garnish, Noah," she cried, but opened her mouth meekly at his glare of exasperation. He held the parsley above her mouth like a plump grape.

"Weren't you listening in your nutrition class? Parsley is a valuable source of vitamin E, which just happens to increase virility." He let the parsley fall into her mouth and winked. "I like virile women."

"Women aren't virile, Noah, men are," Gin retorted as she chewed the herb. "If I continue to eat with you, I'll be fat as well as ill. This is awful!"

"Don't worry, Ginny. I also like my women fat and ill." He reached across the table and took her chin in his hand, and Gin felt wispy butterflies begin to flutter in her middle. It was hard to remain angry at him, no matter what he did. "Fatness and illness eliminate all competition," he explained, moving his hand to lightly caress her cheek.

"Oh, but the grapevine tells me you like slim, dark-haired nurses two to one." Gin moved her head away. The hell with the observers. She had agreed to meet him to voice all her objections, to confront him with his infidelity.

"Ah, yes. My nemesis, the grapevine. Far be it from me to contradict any such facts the grapevine deems valid, no matter how wild or inaccurate they might be." He stood up and leaned across the table and, to her surprise, kissed her again. "Actually," he whispered, "slim, dark-haired nurses drive me into a frenzy of passion."

"Have you seen Catherine Timmits lately?" she asked when he sat back down.

He looked sharply up at her, then calmly took a sip of coffee. "Yes. I drove her to work yesterday. Why do you ask? Something bothering you?"

Gin searched her mind for an appropriate answer, then shook her head. "Nothing really important. I-I left a brooch in the staff lounge the night the Brandner boy was injured. I thought she might have found it." Gin knew she sounded like a jealous shrew. Even to her the excuse she had just given him sounded false. Mature relationships are based on trust, she recalled him saying. But, he had destroyed her trust!

Noah was studying her as if he too were weighing the truth of her words. "I'll ask her about it the next time I see her," he said. "We live in the same apartment building and share rides occasionally when she's on a swing shift."

I'll bet, Gin thought. It amazed her that he could lie so glibly without a trace of guilt. At least her lie had sounded fradulent. His skill must come from years of practice, she mused, looking into the clear, gray eyes that were assessing her so boldly.

"Why don't we slip away somewhere private for a while?" Noah asked softly, his gaze fixed on the swell of her breasts. Gin felt as if he'd undressed her. "Despite that ugly uniform, you're the most desirable creature I've seen today."

"Surely there must have been some nurse who caught your eye," Gin replied dryly, aware that only a thin thread stood between her rational self and her flaring temper.

"Ginny, you puzzle me more than any woman I've ever known. Is something bothering you, or are you just in one of your moods?"

"Where were you last night?" Gin asked, controlling her voice and hoping her question sounded casual. "I waited several hours." Did she really want to hear his answer?

"I don't have the time today for another verbal skirmish with you, and I'm sorry I didn't explain it earlier, Ginny, but I really forgot all about it in the pleasure of seeing you again. I was at the hospital all night, sleeping," he said without hesitation. "Jim Brandner's condition deteriorated yesterday afternoon, and I worked like hell to save him."

"You spent the entire night at the hospital sleeping?" She glared at him, daring him to repeat his obvious lie.

"I'm sorry if you waited. It was touch and go for several hours. I wanted to be close by if they needed me. I fell asleep in the interns' quarters and don't remember a thing past six o'clock. Saving that kid means a lot to me," he continued, his voice now very serious. "I don't know exactly why he's so special to me, but it's almost a personal vendetta against the inequities of life."

"Is he better?" Gin knew Noah wasn't lying about the child's condition or his feelings about saving him, only where he had spent the night. She had called the hospital several times and was told he wasn't there.

"Much improved. It's a good thing, too. I slept so soundly I could have been a corpse. I did miss your nursing skills, though. Had someone of your caliber been on duty, I wouldn't have had to stay."

He was so good at this he even knew all the right things to say to allay her suspicions, Gin thought furiously. Slept like a corpse! Sure! Aloud she said, "Now you're complimenting my skills. I remember when you thought I was incompetent."

He glanced at his watch again and sprang out of the booth. "That's because you were the only woman who had ever challenged my authority. I've got to run, Ginny. Listen, I have to meet with Dr. Abrams tonight to talk about my private practice, so I'll see you tomorrow, okay?" He leaned down and kissed her again, a brief brush of his lips against her cheek. "Your place at eight. Wear something sexy. We'll go to this great romantic spot I know and talk all about this." He turned and strode away before she could answer.

She watched him leave the restaurant, irritated that he had dominated and charmed her into submission while she chafed inside. Knowing him, that romantic spot would be the nearest bed. Well, she was already tired of being useful to Noah Grady. He would never change, and she didn't intend to stick around and be his doormat. Ha! said an inner voice. Just what will you do about it? You must enjoy being dominated. First Nick, now Noah.

Gin pushed her thoughts away and started to gather up her purse and coat, realizing she would be late for work if she didn't hurry. A slip of paper caught her eye, and she stared in astonishment at the check on the table.

"Damn!" she muttered, the uncharacteristic oath escaping from her lips as she fumbled in her purse for her last few dollars. Not only had she suffered through atrocious food and Noah's glib, deceitful company, but she was also stuck with paying the bill!

chapter 9

GIN REGRETTED having called Suzanne that morning.
She wasn't really in the mood for lunch—or for an
inquisition. She had spent most of last night trying
to convince herself that Noah was with Dr. Abrams
instead of with someone else, and she had come to
another decision during those restless hours—one she
intended to keep this time. She looked around the
crowded cafeteria, certain her friend would try to dis-
suade her and determined not to let her.

As Gin slid into the booth, apologizing for her
lateness, Suzanne leaned back to examine her shape-
less, unattractive uniform. "Well, how are things in
the world of generics, tomato soup, and coupons?"

"The computer shut down this morning, and a
woman accused me of cheating because her total was
different from the one on the register tape."

"So it's not all roses and perfume. What did you
expect, Gin?"

"What is this?" Gin asked. "A two-person crusade

to badger me into admitting I was wrong? I don't need your sarcasm too, Suzanne."

"Well, I'm glad you don't have rabies." Suzanne sat back in the booth and sighed as the waitress arrived to take their order and pour coffee.

Gin paused. "I'm sorry. That was really churlish of me. I've been so miserable lately I can't tolerate myself either."

"Mmm, do I detect a note of derision now that you and Noah Grady have finally got this thing going?"

"It's this 'thing' that's bothering me," Gin said, fiddling with a straw wrapper. "I'm thinking of leaving Minnesota."

"So have three million other residents who are frozen right up to their proverbial eyeballs. They're sticking around for the spring thaw, though. So what's your reason?"

"Noah," Gin said simply.

"Well, that certainly sums it up in one word. I'm glad I asked."

"Our relationship," Gin explained further.

"Which should be absolutely, phenomenally happy. Why are you trying to mess it up?"

"Suzanne, whose side are you on?"

"Gin, I'm not terribly brilliant, but it's plain to see Noah Grady thinks you're the greatest thing to happen to him since the scalpel. What's the matter, isn't he GIB? Good in bed," Suzanne explained at Gin's blank look. "You really are slow today."

Gin shook her head unhappily. "I seem to be beset with vows I can't keep and impetuous decisions I regret."

"So don't make any vows or decisions," Suzanne concluded logically. "Let things happen."

"That's just the whole point," Gin said. "Nothing's happened."

"I don't understand, Gin." Suzanne looked puzzled. "You're dating Noah Grady and nothing's happened?"

Gin flushed a deep crimson. "Not that!" she asserted. "I mean nothing meaningful has resulted. I-I—oh, I don't know. I'm so confused. I think I love him, then I remember that only six months ago I was desperately in love with another man. How can I possibly be sure that this isn't just physical attraction or another manifestation of the self-destructive tendencies I recently realized I have?"

"You're skirting the issue, Gin, and you know what they say about a little knowledge. I really don't think you should try self-analysis."

"How's the baby?" Gin changed the subject abruptly, nodding at Suzanne's rotund shape.

"Like an elephant." Suzanne patted her protruding abdomen. In spite of her terse comment, Gin noticed the soft radiance that emanated from her face.

"When is your last night?" Gin looked at her closely, realizing she seemed a bit uncomfortable.

"Tonight. I have a month to pamper myself and get the nursery in order. That is, if I ever get rid of this backache."

"When did the pain start?" Gin prodded, frowning with concern.

"Backache—no pain, and it started early this morning. I swear the little devil is paying me back for all the food I've consumed. I'm ordering cottage cheese today."

"Suzanne, could you be in labor?" Gin asked. "You might have miscalculated."

Suzanne shook her head vigorously as the waitress arrived with their orders. "Not the omnipotent Dr. Boris Miller. He wouldn't make such an error. When I asked him last month about that possibility, my obstetrician extraordinaire said it was most unlikely, but that when the fruit is ripe it will fall from the tree. I shudder to think that in seven years of medical school, internship, and residency that's all he learned," she concluded, giggling.

"Regardless," Gin said, laughing with her friend, "I think you should call in sick."

"What? And have Mrs. Brashler in hysterics?"

"She can always kidnap a warm, breathing body off the street, Suzanne," Gin said, certain now that Suzanne should skip work.

"That doesn't say much for our skills, does it? Don't worry, Gin, I'll make it through. Maybe Grady will send up his med students again."

"Noah sent medical students to the floor to help?" Gin asked, incredulous.

Suzanne nodded, grinning. "You should have seen their faces when I told them to give all the patients backrubs."

They laughed together, then Suzanne leaned back in the booth. "Now that we've exhausted all other avenues of conversation, let's get back to Gin Selton. What exactly is the problem?"

Gin sipped her coffee thoughtfully, then sighed. "I don't know. I'm happy and I'm unhappy. I've got everything any normal woman could possibly want in a man. He's warm, loving, considerate, handsome, successful . . ."

"And drives you absolutely crazy at times," Suzanne finished. "A trait indigenous to the male species. So why the scowl?" Suzanne pushed the cottage cheese around on her plate with distaste.

"He hasn't mentioned love, nor has he made even a remote suggestion of permanence."

"Maybe he's frightened," Suzanne suggested. "Or have you ever considered he's been too busy these past years becoming a success to think about sharing his life with a woman?"

"I could buy the latter theory, Suzanne, but what could he possibly be frightened of? To my knowledge he hasn't suffered unrequited love or any other unfortunate experiences with women."

"The key words there are *to my knowledge*. Maybe you don't really know. Besides, I have another theory."

"Spare me." Gin laughed in spite of the serious tone of their conversation.

"Suffer through. I'm trying to help. Grady's always been a playboy, and you know that type. They tell every woman they see how much they love them just to get them into bed. Perhaps Grady can't verbalize his feelings this time because they're really true." Suzanne seemed confident that her analysis was correct and grinned like a Cheshire cat.

"Suzanne, I think it's fortunate you don't have a couch. What was that you just mentioned about a little bit of knowledge?"

"Okay. How about you? Have you mentioned marriage or love to him?" Suzanne asked.

"No," Gin admitted, throwing her napkin into her plate of food. "I can't."

"And why not? Oh, don't bother to answer. You're so darned proud it's disgusting. Can't you *see* how much he loves you."

"No," Gin answered honestly. "I don't believe Noah is capable of loving a woman, at least not with the same depth that I love him, and he certainly has no intentions of settling down to just *one* woman."

"Okay, so he's never said he loves you. But how about the way he's changed? Even the women in the operating room are talking about it. They want to build a monument to you. Do you believe Grady asked a student nurse to scrub with him the other day so he could teach her about endarterectomies?"

"Was she pretty?" Gin asked in a brusque tone of voice.

"Aha! The green-eyed monster has smitten Gin Selton. Why don't you look in a mirror sometime?"

Gin bit her lip, hoping the physical pain would overcome the emotional one. "He spent Thursday night with Catherine Timmits."

"Stop driving yourself crazy and ask him about it. Maybe it's not what you think."

"I did. He had a convenient excuse."

"So believe it."

"Don't be patronizing, Suzanne. Noah is a man who enjoys the chase. I'm terrified he'll cast me aside one day when he realizes he's made the conquest. I want a home . . . and a family. I want—"

Suzanne glanced at her sharply. "I think you want to believe all this garbage you're telling yourself, but before I pass judgment, let me get it all straight in my addled brain. You've known Noah Grady for about two months. You've dated for"—she looked at her calendar watch—"two weeks, three days, and twenty-five minutes, most of which you've spent quarreling. He's made love to you, has become a living saint around other people, and showers you with attention. Maybe, just maybe, he spent the night with another woman—and so what if he did—but because he hasn't said those magic words, you're running scared. Tell me, Gin, would they really make a difference, or is that just an excuse to run out on him before things get serious? I think you're the one who's afraid of love, my dear."

"Thanks," Gin said with a frown.

"Too close to the truth?" Suzanne asked. "If you ask me, that's why you went out with someone like

Nick Carlin to begin with. He was safe, because deep down you knew he would never fully commit himself to you. You wouldn't have to love him back forever. Grady was safe, too, until things started to get serious."

"I didn't come here to listen to a lecture, Suzanne," Gin said briskly. "I've made up my mind. I don't intend to get hurt again."

"Gin, thousands of women have been hurt. You don't have a patent on it. Life is full of little moments of agony. You pick up the pieces and go on. I can't stand to watch you destroy the beginning of what could be a beautiful relationship. In the brief time I've known you, you've had everything so together. *I'm* the silly, flighty person. You've got to get hold of yourself."

"Which is why I'm leaving," Gin said. "I can't seem to make sense out of my life here."

"Where will you go?" Suzanne pushed her plate away.

Gin shrugged. "I have a friend who used to work as a frontier nurse in Kentucky, but she was a midwife too. I've been thinking about that. But I'd also like to go to Houston and work in open-heart."

"Well, at least you're not considering a career in food management," Suzanne quipped.

"The grocery store hasn't been *that* bad. It's hard work. I've gained a grudging admiration for people who do it, but I also miss medicine. I know I can't return to a typical hospital. I can't stand the restrictions. I want something where I can be totally involved with my patients. Noah was right. There are some things you can't change."

"When are you planning to tell him?" Suzanne turned her glass of milk around on the table, looking at it as if it were full of arsenic.

"Tonight," Gin said, "and I'm not looking forward to it."

Suzanne shook her head sadly. "I think you're making the biggest mistake of your life, Gin Selton, but I'm your friend, and I'll help you all I can." She rubbed her back again and grimaced. "Jeez, you'd think this kid would lay off its mama-to-be, wouldn't you?"

"Friend," Gin said, "I think you'd better visit Dr. Boris Miller right now!"

Gin heard the telephone ringing as she inserted her key into her apartment door. She had spent most of the afternoon at work worrying about both Noah and Suzanne, and now she wondered if the call was from either one of them.

She ran across the room and caught the phone on the third ring. "Hello?" she answered breathlessly.

"Gin? Robert Bonati calling." He sounded tired and incredibly worried.

"How's Suzanne?" Gin asked, already knowing she was in labor.

"Can you come, Gin?" Robert said. "She's upset, and I don't seem to be doing anything right. I hate to ask, but she became hysterical when I offered to call my mother."

"I'll be right there," Gin answered before he could apologize further. "What are friends for? Just give me a few minutes to change."

When Gin walked into the labor room half an hour later, wearing a long green hospital gown over her hastily donned skirt and blouse, she was surprised at Suzanne's emotional state. The woman who had become Gin's close friend was now a nervous wreck. Suzanne had been crying, and her eyes were red-rimmed and wide with fear. Even though Gin's experience in obstetrics was limited, she could see that Suzanne was fighting the contractions instead of relaxing and letting nature take its course.

"Oh, Gin," Suzanne sobbed when she saw her, "I'm so glad you came. I've—I've never had a b-baby before, and I'm so scared."

"Well," Gin said matter-of-factly, "neither have I, but I think we can make it through this if we all work together." She glanced at Robert Bonati, who seemed distraught and looked as if he hadn't slept in days, though Gin knew he and Suzanne had been at the hospital for only a matter of hours.

She grasped Suzanne's hand and squeezed it tightly, smoothing loose strands of hair away from her perspiring forehead. "First of all," Gin said authoritatively, "let's practice breathing."

Bit by bit, Gin remembered scraps of information from her obstetrics rotation in nursing school, and soon Suzanne was able to relax and work with her contractions. Gin smiled confidently when Robert Bonati flashed her a grateful look over the bed and calmly issued orders to her friend as the evening slowly progressed.

When a resident announced that Suzanne's delivery was imminent, Gin could see the gray mist of dawn spread over the city from a nearby window. She was exhausted from the many hours she had sat at Suzanne's side, and her muscles ached in protest as she stretched, preparing to leave. She was surprised when Dr. Miller invited her into the delivery room. She glanced at Suzanne for confirmation. This was, after all, a very private moment—one she didn't want to intrude on without permission.

"You can catch Robert if he faints, Gin." Suzanne gave a half laugh, then a tremulous grin. "We're going to name our little girl Ginelle, so I think you should at least be one of the first to see her."

Gin laughed, and caught Suzanne's hand in a final, encouraging squeeze. "What if it's a boy?" she teased, then turned away to help Robert scrub and gown while Suzanne was transferred to the delivery table.

Only minutes later time seemed suspended as Dr. Miller expertly guided the child into the world. Gin held her breath until the tiny infant screamed his anger at being thrust into the cold Minnesota morning.

"A nice, healthy boy," Dr. Miller proclaimed once the baby had been bundled in warm blankets and placed in Suzanne's arms. He turned the overhead light on her and with a warm smile motioned for Robert to join them.

Gin's heart swelled at the expression of love on their faces. Robert and Suzanne looked down at the miracle they had created, counting fingers and toes, then looking up at each other. The gaze of adoration that passed between them almost overwhelmed Gin. It was the most beautiful moment she had ever witnessed. She realized then that the choice between Texas and Kentucky had just been made for her. She was ready to return to nursing.

Several minutes later Gin stood in front of the nursery windows, staring at blue- and pink-blanketed babies sleeping peacefully in tiny bassinets. Despite the fatigue that was creeping into every bone in her body, Gin felt a soft, warm glow as she watched the changing expressions on the tiny faces. She smiled when a particularly small baby girl who had caught her eye yawned, then squiggled up her mouth, sucking furiously on a tiny fist. She felt an almost empty longing and couldn't help but imagine herself as the mother of her own tiny miracle. Hers and Noah's.

She tried to push the thought from her mind, reminding herself that she was leaving Minnesota—and

Noah. Pretending to be a mother was wishful thinking. Noah had no intention of being tied down to a woman, and his plans certainly didn't include children. Noah wanted a private practice and a chance for the success he had worked so hard to achieve, not a wife and family. Wasn't that one of the reasons she was leaving? Loving a man who didn't love her back, and the prospect of never having a family, were driving her away.

She tore her eyes reluctantly from the babies and turned toward the fathers' waiting room, hoping to get a cup of hot coffee. She still had to face Noah, an encounter she wasn't looking forward to.

"Imagine meeting you here," said a light, feminine voice behind her.

Gin turned to find Mary Anne Harner, looking more darkly sultry and slimmer than ever. Suddenly Gin was conscious of how rumpled her own clothes must look compared to the attractively attired, expertly coiffed woman's. "Yes, imagine meeting you here," Gin echoed politely.

"Are you visiting someone?" Mary Anne seemed to want to prolong the conversation. She peered at the babies behind the broad windows.

"Suzanne Bonati just had her baby," Gin explained, feeling uncomfortable. She pointed to the bassinet where Robert junior was sleeping. "And you?" she felt obligated to ask. Mary Anne was beaming from ear to ear.

"I just came from my gynecologist's office," Mary Anne answered with a cheerful smile. "He informs me that I'm pregnant. I'm on my way to tell the lucky father that it's time to buy a wedding ring." She seemed very happy about her new situation. "Oh, shall I say hello to Noah for you?" she asked, almost as an afterthought. "I'll be seeing him about . . ."

Mary Anne's voice continued, but Gin didn't hear her. *Shall I say hello to Noah for you?* blared in her mind until she wanted to put her hands over her ears and scream with agony. Mary Anne had as much as admitted that Noah was the father of her unborn child!

"N-no," Gin stammered, clenching her hands in front of her. "I-I'll be seeing him soon myself," she said, vaguely remembering that she hadn't left him a note or called him all night.

Gin turned and walked into the staff lounge, surprised to notice how calm she was. She looked down at her hands. They weren't shaking at all. In fact, they were quite still, almost numb.

"Did you see him, Gin? Did you see how big he is?" Robert Bonati asked enthusiastically. Having already poured two cups of coffee, he handed Gin a steaming cup with a proud smile.

"He's a beautiful baby, Robert," Gin assured him. "I can already tell he's going to be a linebacker for the Minnesota Vikings." She smiled at Suzanne's husband. "I think he's got Suzanne's nose."

"Oh, Gin!" Robert almost exploded with joy. "We did it!" He laughed and held his arms wide.

Gin laughed too and went willingly into his arms, crying just a bit on his strong shoulder. "It was incredibly beautiful, Robert," she whispered against his rough coat. "Are you seeing Suzanne again before you leave?"

"Well, isn't this touching," Noah said cynically from the doorway. "Are congratulations in order?" he asked casually, but Gin was aware of the sharpness in his voice.

Robert hardly seemed to notice Noah's sarcasm. Smiling broadly, he vigorously pumped Noah's hand, then stuck a cigarette in his shirt pocket, promising him a cigar as soon as possible. Excusing himself with a wave of his hand and a brief "Thanks again, Gin. See you soon," he hurried off to see Suzanne.

"My first operation was canceled," Noah said as soon as Robert had gone. "Shall we talk at your apartment or mine?"

The harsh timbre of his voice and aloof manner infuriated Gin, and she glared at him and started to speak, then thought better of it. She needed time to control her raging anger. She wanted to end their relationship calmly and rationally so that he would have no reason to misunderstand. She tossed her hair back and swept past him, grabbing her purse and coat. She left quickly, appearing unconcerned about whether he followed or not.

They were both tensely quiet during the short ride to her apartment. Gin concentrated on what she was going to say to him when they arrived, silently reminding herself to keep her self-control once she unleashed her fury on him. She was aware that he was also angry, but she didn't care to question why. She was the injured party!

Noah slammed the apartment door shut behind him and whirled to face her so rapidly that Gin felt almost dizzy. "Where the hell were you?" he rasped, his voice barely controlled. "I waited all night for you and then, when I finally did find you, it was in another man's arms!"

"How dare you insinuate that something is going on between Robert and me!" she exclaimed, realizing she had already lost the battle with her temper. Where in the world did he think she was, and what right did he have to question her? "Robert is a good fr—"

"It's not Robert's motivations I'm worried about," he interrupted, grabing her wrist and pulling her roughly against him.

Gin twisted away from his firm hold, her eyes

flashing fire. "Don't judge me by your own indiscriminate bed-hopping, Grady!" she cried, furious at him for his ugly suspicions and at herself for her treacherous, quicksilver response to his touch. She backed away, a mock smile on her face. "I understand you'll soon be joining Robert's happy status," she said. When he looked blankly at her, she laughed mirthlessly. "Oh, haven't you spoken to Mary Anne Harner yet?" she asked sweetly. "She's pregnant."

"That's not my concern." Noah reached for her again.

"Since you're the father, I should think it would be," Gin said, continuing to back away from him.

"You know as well as I do that's not my child."

"No, I don't know that, Noah, but if it were, would you even care?"

"Of course I would *care*, Ginny. I'm not that much of an ogre, despite what you think. But that doesn't mean I'm ready to claim any illegitimate child as my own." Noah's eyebrows were knitted together, and his lips formed a tight line.

For a brief moment Gin almost believed him. But then other images came to mind—the nurses gossiping about Noah Grady's prowess in bed; Catherine Timmits boasting of how he would return to her soon; Mary Ann Harner answering the phone breathlessly after countless rings, having just left Noah in the bedroom. And Gin remembered Nick Carlin, to whom she had given her heart, only to find him entwined in bed with a naked woman. Renewed hurt and anger rose in Gin in a stifling wave, and she hardened herself to tell Noah what she knew she must tell him.

"I'm leaving Minnesota, Noah," she announced quietly in a voice that trembled with suppressed emotion. "I was going to tell you last night."

"Because of this?" He stared at her aghast. "Or are

you running away from your problems again?" he demanded sarcastically. "Try facing the truth for once, Ginny. I doubt you'll find a solution until you do."

"I suppose that in your infinite wisdom you have all the answers," Gin snapped back. "After all, you're a bastion of honesty. Between you and Suzanne I've listened to all the incredible theories about my mixed-up psyche that I can tolerate."

Noah paced the floor in long, restless strides before turning abruptly to her and grasping her arm in an iron grip. "I don't have any more theories, Ginny, but I do have another proposition that might suit both our needs," he said, reaching into his pocket with his other hand. "The detail man from Sevenal Drugs was here, and this gave me an idea that might be a resolution to both our problems." He held out a slim pocket flashlight.

"Grady, I have a whole drawer full of those," Gin said sarcastically.

"I made you an offer a few nights ago," he continued. "I—"

"And if you recall," she broke in quickly, "I haven't accepted your offer." She was struggling to maintain control, but managed to keep her voice cool and aloof.

"There was a particular clause I wanted to revise," he continued as if she hadn't spoken. "You've already enjoyed the fringe benefits, while I've collected little from our unspoken agreement in the way of tenderness and caring. Every time I've needed you, you've been either angry or gone."

"I don't owe you a thing, Grady, but how are you suggesting we rectify that inequitable condition?" She wanted to lash out at him with a thousand accusations, but instead she clenched her hands at her sides. He would only accuse her of having hysterics.

Noah started to pace the floor again, walking back and forth with his hands behind his back and staring intently at the rug. "I've thought this through very carefully," he said. "I've always believed marriage should be approached in a businesslike manner. We have valid reasons for needing each other. I need someone to cook and clean for me, and I desperately need a good, loyal nurse for my office. Therefore I'm willing to forgo my bachelorhood for the state of matrimony. I admit it would be a sacrifice for us both, but it would also be a convenient solution to our problems."

"Grady . . . are—are you . . . *proposing* to me?" Gin asked, incredulous.

Noah gave an offhand shrug. "I guess that's what you could call it. Do you accept?"

"You need a maid with a nurse's license, Grady, not a wife. But at the risk of feeling utterly foolish by pursuing this conversation, I really don't see anything in your proposition that would benefit me."

"As the wife of a highly respected doctor you would never have to worry about supporting yourself. As my nurse you would be able to return to your profession, which you admit you want to do."

Gin shook her head. "I'm sure there are easier ways of supporting myself, even in nursing, than entering into a loveless marriage."

He had moved in front of her and placed his hands on her shoulders. "Emotional declarations don't always cement the bonds of matrimony, Ginny. Sometimes they only gnaw at the foundations. I've never claimed to love any woman, and you insist you're still in love with Nick Carlin, so emotion needn't be a consideration in our agreement."

Gin looked up to meet his silvery gaze. So much for Suzanne's conjecture that Noah loved her, she thought, aware that she had wanted to believe her friend's wild speculations. "There should be something . . ."

"Why? So that two people can make each other miserable? You can do that without love, or you can make something work."

"Even if I were to agree to this . . . arrangement, there's still the matter of Mary Anne's child," Gin said, searching his face for some sign that he cared despite his words. "Shouldn't you be proposing to her?"

"I'm not trying to shirk my responsibilities, if that's what you think, Ginny, but no nurse gets herself pregnant unless she's foolish, stupid, or trying to trap a man." A tiny muscle in his cheek began to twitch, but other than that small sign he seemed to be unaffected by the conversation. "She is not pregnant with my child," he said with such certainty that once again she began to wonder if maybe he was telling the truth. He continued to hold her, staring down at her face as if he could convince her by sheer force of will.

Gin grew uncomfortable under his scrutiny. She trembled slightly and closed her eyes to prevent him from seeing the stark truth of her love for him that she was sure shone there. Even if he was telling the truth this time, she couldn't let him see that she loved him. And she certainly couldn't accept his ridiculous marriage proposal.

"What you're suggesting would be a farce, Noah." She could hardly force the words from her lips, her throat was so choked with emotion. "Marriage isn't something I take lightly."

"Nor I," he said, running his hands down her arms. "But we can work at it. We're compatible, and surely you won't try to deny the attraction between us."

Had she been capable of reacting, Gin would have

ojected to his kiss, but she was immediately swept up in the intense desire she always felt at his expert touch. Before she could move, he had pulled her against him, his lips seeking, bruising, scorching her own with ravaging flames of passion.

Gin moaned deep in her throat, realizing somehow, despite her lack of rational thought, that she was helpless to fight the onslaught of desire that raged in every fiber of her body. She collapsed against his chest, becoming soft and pliable in his arms.

Apparently sensing her unconditional surrender, Noah kissed her again, a deep, lingering caress. He moved one hand slowly down her back and around to the soft curve of her breast, making her shudder with desire. "God, Ginny," he said, his voice husky. "I can't seem to get enough of you. It's like being addicted to a drug. The more I make love to you, the more I want you."

He unbuttoned her blouse slowly and slipped it off her shoulders, his hands seeming to be everywhere at once. Spasms of pleasure coursed through her already heated body when he drew her to him again, his lips moving softly up her throat and across to her mouth as his hands moved over her body, touching, seeking.

"Ginny, you're so beautiful," he whispered hoarsely. The husky quality of his voice made her quiver with uncontrollable longing. She was hardly aware of it when he picked her up and lay her down on the soft pillows of the bed. Somehow he had managed to divest himself of his own clothes; the remainder of hers lay in a heap on the bed. And then he possessed her with a fierceness that left her breathless. Tides of passion seized her, sending her into a spinning, whirling vortex of sensation, until she was no longer aware of anything but the force of his desire and her own awesome response to him.

* * *

Afterward she was consumed by a self-loathing so great that it transcended any other emotion she had ever felt. It left her pale with humiliation. She had been a slave to her own primitive passions, and that fact disgusted her. She had allowed Noah to make love to her, had eagerly encouraged him by responding so fully, even though she knew he would never love her.

As Noah dressed she counted the minute squares the sun, shining through the open-weave draperies, made on her ceiling. She tried to make her mind a void, blinking at the bright light of a new day and thinking it odd that the sky wasn't gray and overcast to match her emotions.

"Ginny?" Noah said softly beside her.

"Yes," she answered dully, turning to face him. He was fully dressed and stood beside the bed, his expression unreadable. She stared at the fine lines around his eyes, the taut skin that stretched over his cheekbones, the straight nose and sensitive lips, trying to commit his face to memory.

"Jim Brandner died yesterday," he said at last.

A wave of sadness washed away her own misery.

"I'm so sorry, Noah. It must have been difficult for you," she mumbled. She fell silent, thinking that the world seemed to be filled with tragedy—her own and other people's.

"Why did you ask me to marry you, Noah?" The question surprised her. She hadn't meant to verbalize her unconscious thoughts.

"Ginny...I..." He looked searchingly at her, running his hand impatiently through his thick dark hair, struggling for words to express an emotion, a thought she could not guess at. Then his expression became closed again, and he reached down to gently caress her cheek. "I'm late. I'll see you tonight," he said, and there was no hint of hesitation in his voice.

When she heard the door to her apartment close, Gin swung her legs over the side of the bed. She showered and dressed carefully, selecting a comfortable traveling suit. When she had thrown a few dresses and essential toilet articles into a suitcase, she walked purposefully to the phone, dialing first the airlines, then Robert Bonati.

After surrendering her key and an extra month's rent to the superintendent, Gin walked out the front door and into the bright sunshine. For a few moments she stared down at the melting patches of ice on the sidewalk and at the dark grime marring piles of snow that had been white and clean just a few nights ago. She sighed and walked quickly away, hoping never to see another snowflake for as long as she lived.

chapter 10

GIN PLACED her head in her hands and clenched her
jaw tight, fighting the nausea that threatened to spill
up into her throat. She inhaled slowly, then, when the
wave of bile subsided somewhat, opened a package
of soda crackers. Nibbling on a cracker, she wandered
over to the tall window on the far side of her office
and looked out at the towering hills in the distance.

Spring was coming early to this part of the Appalachians. Already the trees were greening and
sprouting with new life. The hard, reddish soil was
bulging with moisture to support the riot of bloom
that would soon spring forth. A mockingbird perched
in a giant sycamore tree caught her eye as he shrilled
outside the window, his imitation of a crow reminding
Gin of the sour disposition she'd had during the past
few weeks.

She sighed and let the drape fall back into place,
then almost ran to the sink, taking slow, deep breaths
to keep from retching. Clutching the cold porcelain,

she lifted her head to stare at her reflection in the small mirror.

Her hair hung limp and lifeless around her face, and deep circles shadowed her eyes. She stepped back for a detailed self-examination. She had lost too much weight, she decided, then a wry thought occurred to her—she would soon be gaining it all back.

What had happened to the starry-eyed woman who had gazed into a mirror only two months ago? She'd found out she was pregnant, that's what, she answered herself. She regretted having allowed her passion for Noah Grady to overcome her good sense, but another part of her reveled in the thought of bringing his child into the world. Noah would never return her love for him, but the child she carried would go a long way toward making up for that loss. She loved the child already.

Suddenly Gin retched again but, determined not to vomit, she sipped a glass of water. "Nausea during pregnancy is only encountered in highly sophisticated societies," she recalled her professor stating just yesterday. "Studies have proven that in America it is endemic among most socioeconomic groups except for the very poor, and it is most definitely emotional, more than likely a ploy by the woman to gain attention from her mate."

Gin frowned at her reflection, then wriggled her nose and stuck out her tongue. "That can't be my problem," she said aloud. "I don't have a mate!"

"Are you all right, Gin?" Douglas Whitney called from the doorway. "You look awful."

"Oh! You startled me, Douglas." Gin turned toward the middle-aged man who had befriended her the moment she had walked into Whitney Clinic six weeks ago to apply for a job as a frontier nurse. He had been a great source of comfort and support, always there when she needed him.

"Why don't you skip classes this afternoon," he suggested, frowning. "The drive into Hyden is long, and you look as if you could use some rest."

Gin shook her head. "If they're willing to give me a course in midwifery in three months, the least I can do is show up. I'll be fine, Douglas. Don't worry."

"Well, be careful on these roads. You still don't handle the Jeep very well. And I hired you as a family clinician. You don't really have to take the course in midwifery."

"Douglas, you've been kind enough to make me a partner in Whitney Clinic. I can help more if I improve my skills, and I've discovered that midwifery is a necessity here."

He studied her seriously. "You handled Cassie Laughton very well, despite the fact that you're not a midwife. I'm content with the knowledge you've brought to Whitney Clinic."

"Believe me, Douglas, Cassie Laughton survived by the sheer force of my will. There weren't any skills involved, just lots of prayer and determination." Gin could laugh now, but she remembered the frantic efforts she had made to staunch the hemorrhaging after the precipitous birth of Cassie's third child. A month later the baby was still hospitalized in Middlesboro, but Cassie had come home two weeks ago and had thanked Gin nonstop ever since.

"Nevertheless, I'm happy with your performance so far. Only one thing bothers me," he said, smiling down at her.

"What's that?" Gin asked, concerned that he was troubled by something she might have done.

"You keep refusing to cry on my shoulder. I've told you before that it's quite large and always well padded." He gave her a fatherly scowl.

"I don't have time for tears, Douglas," Gin said briskly. Nor for this darned nausea, she thought as her stomach did another flip-flop.

Douglas caught her hands in his. "Will you have time for your unborn child?" he asked.

"How—how did you know I was pregnant?" she whispered, surprised. She had been agonizing over how he would accept her news, but he seemed to be simply and sincerely concerned.

"I'm an obstetrician and gynecologist, Gin. I've seen literally thousands of pregnant women in my forty-plus years. Although I tell my patients their symptoms aren't confirmation, there are certain ways of telling, and I pride myself on recognizing them." Douglas sat down in the chair opposite her desk and placed his hands behind his head. "For instance, haven't you ever noticed how a pregnant woman often places her hands over the lower portion of her abdomen in an unconscious gesture of protection? It's as if she's shielding the fetus from harm. You do that a lot, Gin. And then there are body changes—enlarged breasts, fatigue, dark circles under the eyes, and, of course, nausea, which seems to have plagued you especially. Are you that upset about the baby?"

Gin sat down opposite him and flashed him a tolerant grin. "It seems to me that all the people who believe in the emotional causes of nausea during pregnancy are males who have never experienced the rigors of childbearing. No, I'm not upset about the baby," she said, then immediately contradicted herself. "That's not quite true. I *am* upset about my lack of judgment in the recent past, but don't worry, I already love this child very much."

"Gin, this may be none of my business, and if I'm intruding where I shouldn't, just say so. But you know I think of you as the daughter I lost many years ago. I care very much about you." Douglas seemed to be searching for the right words, which was unusual for him. "Have you told the father yet?" he finally asked.

"Thank you for your concern, Douglas," Gin told him warmly. "Your daughter would have been a very lucky girl. How did you survive all the terrible tragedies in your life?"

"I see you're changing the subject. Does that mean this is none of my business?" Douglas shoved his hands into his trouser pockets, a wry expression on his face.

"It means I haven't told the father yet, and I don't intend to," Gin admitted.

"Are you prepared for the consequences of bearing a child out of wedlock, Gin?" Douglas asked, obviously deeply concerned. "It's unfortunate, but even today, in our tolerant society, there's a stigma attached to illegitimacy."

"I'm sure it won't be easy, Douglas, but I don't really have a choice. The father doesn't care, and I suspect he never did."

"I can't believe that." Douglas shook his head. "Surely he's not as awful as you make him seem, otherwise why would you have loved him?"

"Perhaps I didn't love him," Gin replied, turning to a chart to hide her expression. She didn't want to talk about Noah, especially not to Douglas.

"I find that hard to believe, Gin. You're not the type of woman who gives herself up to mere physical attraction."

"Thanks for the vote of confidence, Douglas, but that's the way it happened." Gin frowned, then turned back to him and continued. "Noah made it quite clear that if I had harbored any hopes of him loving me, they were just wishful thinking. I'm sure he's happily pursuing his bachelorhood and private medical practice. Of course, if he really wants to claim a child, another one of his lovers is also anticipating motherhood." She turned her attention back to the chart, hoping he understood that as far as she was concerned the subject was closed.

Douglas sighed and shook his head. "Would you like a prescription for the nausea? You can't stand to lose much more weight. As you know, this first trimester is very important to the development of the fetus."

"No, thanks, I'll survive," Gin assured him with a bright smile.

"Stubborn and proud to the end, I see," Douglas said.

Gin laughed. "You make them sound like such unendearing qualities."

"No, not unendearing, just frustrating to most members of the male population. I'll tell you what. Let's go for a hike up Big Bunyan this afternoon. I think the bluebells might be in bloom, and besides, the exercise will stimulate your appetite."

Big Bunyan was the mountain just across the highway, affectionately nicknamed by the members of the clinic because of its imposing size. Gin nodded. "You're on." A hike in the mountains might be just what she needed. "Just as soon as I get back from Hyden," she amended, rising from her desk and kissing him affectionately on the cheek. "Thanks, Douglas," she said. "I appreciate your concern."

"Every time I look for you I find you in the arms of another man," a cold familiar voice from the doorway interjected.

Gin inhaled sharply, then froze. She would have recognized that mocking, sexy voice anywhere. She felt the blood drain from her face, and the nausea she had conquered a few minutes before returned with sudden, sickening force. She whirled to face him.

"H-hello, Noah," she managed to stammer. If possible, he looked even more handsome than she remembered, but his face had the same confident smirk that had never failed to irritate her.

Douglas rose from his chair, his glance going from Gin's pale face to Noah Grady, who had assumed a deceptively casual stance, and back again. If he recognized the name, he didn't give any indication of it. He held his hand out in a friendly gesture. "Douglas Whitney," he introduced himself.

"Noah Grady," Noah muttered, extending his hand and glaring at Gin over Douglas's shoulder at the same time.

They stood in tense silence for a moment, then Douglas cleared his throat and moved toward the door. "This looks like a private conversation," he said. "I'll be in my office if you need me, Gin." He turned and closed the door. The soft click seemed to echo prophetically in the sudden stillness.

Gin nervously clasped her hands in front of her and swallowed with effort. Then, when she could command her legs to move, she sat down in the chair behind her desk and looked at Noah from behind a haughty mask. "How's Mary Anne?" she asked, keeping her voice steady with effort. She would not allow him to see how his mere presence was affecting her.

"Happily married to Dr. David Michaels," Noah answered in tightly controlled, clipped tones. "I was best man."

"How nice," Gin managed to murmur. "It was kind of Dr. Michaels to save you from the trap of fatherhood."

She turned to a chart in a gesture of dismissal, then gasped in surprise when Noah grabbed the chart from her hands and slammed it down on the desk. He leaned across the desk, his expression thunderous. "That child wasn't mine, but this one is! Why didn't you tell me you were pregnant?" He enunciated each word clearly, his voice low and ominous.

Gin stared at him in astonishment. Suzanne must have told him, she thought quickly, then realized there was no sense in denying it. He obviously knew the truth. "I thought you were too busy entertaining every nurse at Lakeside General to care," she answered sarcastically, drawing back from his furious scowl.

Noah took a seat opposite her, crossing one leg over the other, his heel resting on his knee. His foot jabbed the side of her desk impatiently. "I didn't travel over eight hundred miles to this godforsaken coal-mining town in the middle of nowhere to listen to your adolescent ravings, Ginny," he said with ominous control.

"Then why did you come, Noah?" she queried with feigned unconcern. "I certainly didn't invite you."

He placed his hands behind his head and stared at her, openly daring her to challenge his words. "To take you back to Minnesota."

"Then it's too bad you made such a long trip," Gin replied. "I have no intention of returning."

"That happens to be my child you're carrying, and you will return with me!" He brought his foot to the floor with an emphatic thud. "We'll get married as soon as we arrive back."

Gin glared at him furious. "You really surprise me, Noah. I thought you didn't go around claiming illegitimate children as your own. Your image of success doesn't include a family."

"I'll manage to make the sacrifice this time," he said, glaring back at her.

"Your self-immolation is touching," she replied in a haughty tone. "But no thanks."

He stared at her thoughtfully. "Surely you don't intend to deny your child its father, or have you fooled another man into believing it's his?" He jerked his head toward the door. "Douglas Whitney seemed awfully concerned to be just a friend."

His slur surprised and infuriated her. "Douglas has been very kind to me. Please don't involve him in your twisted assumptions!"

Noah jumped up from the chair, rounded the desk, and grasped her arm, jerking her up against his long, hard body. "I'll just bet! And has his kindness extended to your bedroom?"

Gin gasped at the cruelty of his remark. "Get out!" she cried. "I refuse to listen to your ugly innuendos!" She forced herself to meet his eyes.

Noah smiled and ran a hand slowly down the length of her back and over the curve of her hip. "Anger becomes you," he said in a low, husky tone. "Your cheeks glow and your eyes flash fire." He started to bring his lips down to hers, and she felt helpless to prevent it. Despite her anger and his arrogance, an almost overwhelming desire like liquid heat had spread through her body.

Fool, her mind screamed. She was a fool for giving in to passion, for still loving him. She twisted out of his grip and stalked over to the file cabinet, pulling out several charts. Physical activity usually helped to contain her rage. Her response to him had humiliated her, especially because the twinkle in his eyes more than confirmed the fact that he had been aware of her desire.

"I'm not leaving without you, Ginny. You may as well accept that," he said when she sat back down at her desk.

Gin slammed the charts down on the shiny wood, but managed to control her voice. She refused to lower herself further by shouting at him. "Noah, you haven't cared about me or this child in the past few weeks. Why the sudden interest?"

"Despite what you may think, I intend to be a father to my child," he answered, calm now, but Gin noticed a tiny muscle twitching in his cheek.

"I suppose you expect me to believe that." It took supreme effort, but Gin kept her voice in check. "You don't have to salve your conscience, Noah. I can manage alone."

"You can't manage a thing alone, Ginny!" he snapped, rising from the chair once again and leaning over her desk. "You're so intent on running from life and lying to yourself that you wouldn't recognize the truth if it were thrust in front of you. You're too stubborn to open your eyes and—"

Gin slammed her hands down on the desk and rose to face him. "I'm sick and tired of your arrogance!" she exclaimed. "You're so damned perfect, you never make a mistake, Noah Grady! Why don't you just wallow in your smug superiority and leave other people alone!"

Noah took a deep breath and sat down. "Hurling accusations at each other isn't going to accomplish much, Ginny," he said calmly. "Sit down and let's talk quietly and rationally about this situation."

When Gin sat back down in her chair, Noah looked around her office as if he had just realized where they were. He picked up a wooden nameplate and turned it over in his hands. "I see you're back in nursing," he said, placing the nameplate back on her desk. "Do the patients pay for their services with poultry? Or are all those movies about poverty-stricken Appalachian towns exaggerated?"

Gin mentally counted to ten before replying to his condescending question. "Noah, I'm going to ignore your slur. I've finally found my place in medicine here at Whitney Clinic. These people may be poor, but they're wealthy in ways that you wouldn't understand. I have my own patients. I'm responsible for their entire care, and I've been accepted by the community. They may not be able to pay me with money, but there are other rewards in this job, and I'm very happy. In fact, my patients' gratitude has been very humbling. Perhaps you should try something other than big-city neurosurgery. It might help improve your attitude."

Noah rose from his chair once again and began pacing the floor. "Is there somewhere private where we can talk, Ginny?" he asked, looking at her with a pleading expression.

In spite of her anger, Gin could already feel her resolve begin to weaken, and she steeled herself to resist him. "I'm not that much of a fool, Noah. I've learned my lesson." She shook her head. "I don't intend to go anywhere near a bed with you."

"I'm not going to rape you, Ginny. I don't imagine I would have to," he added, reminding her unnecessarily of her earlier response to his casual caress.

"Grady! You're . . ." she began loudly, then lowered her voice when she noticed his cocked eyebrow and wide grin. He had purposely goaded her into losing her temper. "We can talk here, Noah," she said more calmly. "I'm not going anywhere with you, and certainly not to a private place where you can turn on your charm."

He looked around her office. "Do you have any coffee?" he asked. "I've had a long, tiring trip."

Gin sighed and pushed back her chair. "You never give up, do you? There's a restaurant right down the road." It was probably a lot safer than her office anyway, she thought. For a moment she had thought he might try to seduce her right there. "We can talk in a quiet booth," she continued. "But I warn you, that's as far as I'm going with you. We will not under any circumstances go to my apartment."

Gin stuck her head into Douglas's office to let him know where she was going, then tossed a sweater over her shoulders. She let Noah guide her into the street, his hand resting lightly on her back, and inhaled the spring air, suddenly aware of the delightful odors wafting from flower beds on either side of the front steps. Stealing a glance at Noah's tall physique, she acknowledged that whenever she was with him the world around her seemed more vibrant and alive.

She shook the thought from her head and walked beside him, matching her strides to his longer, impatient ones. By the time they arrived at the restaurant, she was slightly out of breath. Aside from her pregnancy, she still hadn't adjusted to walking up and down the steep hills of Sandy Point, especially beside a man who moved with such athletic ease.

When they were settled in a booth near the back of the café, Noah studied a menu. Without bothering to consult her, he ordered a huge country breakfast for himself and two poached eggs, a steak, medium rare, a very large glass of milk, and some raw vegetables for her. Replacing the menu in the napkin holder, he folded his arms across his chest and sat back, fully at ease.

His eyes flicked briefly over Gin's gaunt face. "You look terrible," he said. "You aren't taking care of yourself."

"You may as well have announced to the entire valley that I'm pregnant!" Gin said, looking around the restaurant. She was mortified by the knowing grin the waitress had just flashed her. "People here gossip. By this afternoon it will be common knowledge to every one of my patients."

Noah sipped the hot coffee the waitress had brought and stared at her over the rim of his cup. "I assumed that, since you were willing to face this alone, gossip no longer bothered you."

Gin fidgeted in her seat, determined not to let him goad her into another angry response, and reached into her purse for a cracker. The odor of frying bacon assailed her nostrils, bringing a fresh wave of nausea to plague her. She looked down at the scarred table and gave a small sigh. Being with Noah was like traveling at breakneck speeds, then suddenly shifting into reverse. It was so confusing!

Noah watched her take small bites of the cracker, then reached across the table to grasp her hands. He gave them a slight squeeze as if he were commiserating with her. "How have you been, Ginny?" he asked, his voice a low caress.

He had just changed gears. Gin stared up at him, fully aware of the intense magnetism that still existed between them. She had left Minnesota, but conquering her love for this man was going to be a more difficult task than merely walking out of his life. Even now she felt light-headed whenever he looked at her in that special way of his, and the fluttering in her stomach when he touched her was more than she could bear. She extracted her hand from his grip and took a sip of milk. "I've been fine, Noah," she murmured. "And you?"

"I've finished my residency," he said, leaning back in the booth. "And I've missed you terribly."

"I have to admit, Noah, you're quite good at this. You almost seem sincere. But I still find it hard to believe you."

"Have your experiences made you so distrustful, or do you just enjoy being miserable?" Noah asked.

Ignoring his question, she asked, "Did you find a nurse?" As the waitress placed their food in front of them, she steeled herself for his answer. She *knew* he'd found plenty of them, and they weren't necessarily employees, either.

"Not yet. I haven't decided where to set up my office. I'm still considering several places." Noah stared at the glob of white mush beside his bacon and eggs. "Do they serve this with every meal?"

Gin picked up her fork and started to eat her eggs.

"Those are grits. They're really quite good with butter and salt. In the evening you get fried hominy and a combination of mustard and collard greens boiled with salt pork."

Noah shrugged and dug into his meal. "I can hardly wait to taste the greens."

"Are you planning to stay that long?" Gin asked, staring openly at the chiseled features she had thought never to see again. She wondered now if she had a right to deny her unborn baby its father. Could she raise a child alone subjected to the prejudices of a small, close-knit community? She loved Noah, but how could they make a marriage work when he didn't love her?

"I wasn't planning on staying more than a few hours, but I can see now that it's going to take quite a bit of my charm to convince you to return with me," he answered, making her search her memory for her original question.

Oh yes, she reminded herself. Noah could be charming, devastatingly so. As well as insolent and unfaithful and extremely irritating. "I think I can save you the trouble of delaying your trip, Noah," she told him. "I can't leave Sandy Point. My profession means too much to me, and besides, our relationship would only destroy me in the end."

"Our relationship has barely begun, Ginny. Can't you give it a chance? You're pregnant with my child, and I'm offering to marry you."

Gin struggled with her conflicting feelings. She loved him desperately, but he was offering a marriage of convenience, not love. She had made one mistake by getting pregnant in the first place. Wouldn't she simply be compounding the mistake if she married him?

"It wouldn't work, Noah," she finally said. "You're too arrogant and I'm too stubborn. Neither of us claims to love the other, and I'm still adamant about not getting married for any reason other than love."

"I suppose now you're going to tell me you're still in love with Nick?" he said, cocking a disbelieving eyebrow at her.

Gin blinked in confusion, realizing she hadn't thought of Nick Carlin in weeks. Her entire being had been focused on forgetting Noah. "It's difficult to forget a man you once loved," Gin said truthfully. *That man is you,* she wanted to scream, but she bit her lower lip to keep from blurting out the truth. "You can return to Minnesota with a clear conscience, Noah, if that's what's bothering you."

Gin studied his face intently, her heart constricting with pain. He had offered to marry her again, but for all the wrong reasons. Was she foolish to refuse? No. He didn't love her. He would never love just one woman. And even if she did consider returning with him, he would only be a provider and father to her child. He would be too wrapped up in his new medical practice, too involved in gaining the symbols of success, to pay much attention to her and the baby. He might even begin to resent them both for taking up so much time and money. Despite the fact that she loved him and that she was carrying his child, she couldn't return to Minnesota and face a one-sided relationship. Perhaps she was acting out of stubborn pride, but she deserved more than mere consideration from him.

Noah stared at her. "Why don't you grow up, Ginny, and face facts for a change? I'm offering you the security of marriage and a name for your unborn child, and you tell me that your profession and the memories of a man who's long gone are enough to keep you deliriously happy in this hick town?"

"This hick town happens to be my home," Gin retorted. "You don't really care about me or this child.

You just can't admit to yourself that I'm one of the few women who has ever been able to resist Noah Grady."

"You're a hard case, Ginny and I'm growing tired of arguing with you."

Their voices had risen, and Gin knew the waitress was listening to their conversation with baited breath."Then leave, Noah," she said through clenched teeth. "I can't understand your burning desire to change your marital status anyhow."

"You told me once that even Don Juan had a sense of honor. So do I. Marrying you is one of the more honorable things I've ever offered to do."

"And the last time I saw you you said any nurse who gets herself pregnant is either foolish, stupid, or trying to trap a man. Which category do I fall into?"

"Neither. You're behaving more like a willful, petulant child." He flashed her that indolent grin of his. "Tell the truth just once, Ginny, if only to yourself. Have you been able to forget what it's like between us? You practically smolder when I touch you."

Gin's hands itched to slap his face, but she clenched her teeth and sucked her breath in hard. No longer caring who heard, she rose from the booth and slung her purse over her shoulder, accidently knocking over her glass of milk. "Damn it, Grady!" she said, almost blinded by the red haze of rage in front of her eyes. "I wouldn't marry you if I had leprosy and that were the only known cure! I'm going to Hyden. I'm late for class. I expect you to be gone when I return!"

"Go ahead and run off, Ginny, but this is one time you're going to have to face your problems. I'll be waiting in your office."

"You can wait in hell for all I care, Noah Grady. And as for facing my problems, if they include you, I'd rather risk an encounter with Satan himself." She stalked away, her sharp heels clicking on the linoleum floor.

Driving into the neighboring town, Gin tried to concentrate on the twisting, winding roads, but the image of Noah sitting in the booth with milk dripping onto his lap kept nudging her consciousness. Although it had been an accident, the incident had made her feel terrible.

When she'd looked at him in that moment, she'd thought she'd seen a mixture of admiration and desire on his face. Now she dismissed the expression as inconsequential and braked for a hairpin curve, shifting the Jeep into second, ignoring the grinding of the gears. To Noah she was just a challenge, and she'd never be anything more!

During the next few hours, Gin tried to listen to her professor, but his voice droned on and on while her thoughts tumbled about in confusion. Noah's words echoed over and over in her head. Could his appearance possibly mean he cared for her after all, she kept wondering. He wouldn't have traveled so far to find her just because she was pregnant or because of wounded pride. Perhaps he was also stubborn and proud and couldn't admit that he cared.

Was Suzanne right after all? Noah had spent ten years pursuing a goal. He hadn't had time to consider love. Was his offhand offer of marriage a way of saying "I love you?"

Pushing her thoughts away, she tried to concentrate on the pelvic diagram in her textbook, but within moments she found herself staring out the window, deep in thought once again. Could she trust him? She wanted to with every fiber of her being. She wanted to grow old at his side. She wanted his children. She loved him so much that all the hurt he had subjected her to in the past seemed irrelevant now.

Gin gathered her purse and sweater and bolted from the room. The drive into Sandy Point was the longest she had ever endured. She wanted to fly to Noah's side. She had to reach him! She would say yes to him, would return to Minnesota as his wife. She would miss her patients and her profession, but hadn't women given up goals in the past to follow the man they loved? Surely she could do the same.

Gin rushed to her office and pushed open the door, ready to blurt out her feelings. But the room was empty. For a brief time she had convinced herself that he cared. Now she had to face the final, inevitable, painful truth.

Gin fell into a chair, staring into space. Noah's commanding presence seemed to linger in the room. Once again he had managed to upset her life. Why did she constantly set herself up for rejection? Did she enjoy the hurt?

When Douglas entered her office, Gin glanced up, trying to collect her fragmented thoughts. "Hello," she said with forced cheerfulness, plastering a bright smile on her face.

"Ready for that walk?" Douglas asked, matching her cheerful smile.

"Yes." Gin picked up her charts and walked toward the file cabinet. "You didn't happen to see Noah before he left, did you?" she inquired, hoping against all reason that he was waiting somewhere else for her.

"Yes," Douglas said softly. "He said to tell you he couldn't stay to taste the greens. He mumbled something about a cure for leprosy."

Gin whirled around to look at her partner. "So much for the father of my child," she murmured to herself, then gave Douglas a philosophical shrug. "He didn't like the hominy grits."

Douglas frowned at her for a long moment before

drawing in a deep breath. "Before we go I have some papers for you to sign. You know I've been hiring some new doctors. Now the lawyers are pressing me for the agreements. As a junior partner, your signature is also required."

"Sure," Gin said, welcoming any diversion that would keep her mind off Noah. "Sorry to have held up progress."

After she had scrawled her name on several papers, they headed up Big Bunyan. Gin hardly noticed the budding azaleas and tiny bluebells, so lost was she in her own thoughts. If Noah had cared, she told herself over and over, he would have stayed to try to convince her.

"You love him very much, don't you Gin?" Douglas said, taking her arm and helping her over a fallen log.

Gin stopped and looked around her at the thick trees and dense shrubbery, then tossed her hair back over her shoulders. "Am I that transparent?" she asked with a harsh laugh. "Unrequited love is a dull subject, Douglas. Noah Grady is part of my past, and I prefer to keep it that way."

She turned and continued up the narrow path, brushing the branches of trees aside. She was surprised to realize that she felt almost calm. If only she felt rage or pain or hate. Those tangible emotions she could deal with. But this calmness, this icy control that possessed her body, was pure agony.

chapter 11

THE SLEEK, steel-gray Mercedes should have warned
her, but when Gin noticed it parked in front of the
clinic, she assumed it belonged to a patient from
nearby Sandy Point Heights, a community of wealthy
families who had discovered the peace and beauty of
the Kentucky foothills. Their palatial mansions sprawled
onto neighboring mountainsides, providing a sharp
contrast with the poverty of the valley, and it especially rankled Gin that the roadster's occupant would
flagrantly violate the no-parking-zone regulations just
because the car was so different from the beat-up
trucks and autos jammed into the back lot.

With a tiny jump, she alighted from her Jeep, having discovered several weeks ago that there was no
graceful way to enter and exit such a vehicle, then
sauntered toward the front door, stopping along the
way to admire a dogwood in full bloom. She remembered last noticing the flowering tree two weeks ago,
the day Noah...Gin glanced toward Big Bunyan in
an effort to exorcise the image of Noah Grady from
her mind.

Spring had arrived. Everywhere she looked a riot

of blooms waved in the gentle breeze. In spite of the
mud, brought on by recent heavy rains, that oozed
from cracks and crevices in the hard mountain soil,
Gin was awed by the beauty of the area. During the
past few weeks she had been so intent on forgetting
Noah's sudden return to her life, and his equally sudden exit, that she had failed to notice nature's annual
rebirth.

Promising herself she would take a pleasant walk
in the woods today, Gin slung her purse over her
shoulder and hurried up the front steps into the clinic.

'H'llo, Miz Gin,' Jim Laughton drawled, stepping
down from his ladder to hold the door open for her.

"Hi, Jim. How's Cassie?" Gin paused for a moment
to exchange pleasantries with the handyman.

Jim beamed with pride. "Doin' right fine. We
bringin' the little tyke home next week, thanks to
you."

Gin smiled back at him. Jim Laughton had helped
to win her acceptance from the predominantly coal-
mining and farming community, and she was grateful
to him. The mountain people were usually suspicious
and didn't ordinarily visit doctors and nurses, but Jim
had made certain that every family in the valley knew
Gin had saved his wife as well as his baby son. "I
can hardly wait to see him," Gin said.

Jim narrowed his eyes at her. "You're lookin' right
pretty today," he said. "Feelin' better too, I suspect,"
he added.

Although nothing had been said, Gin was aware
of the rumors that were circulating in the valley about
her condition, and she felt two bright spots of color
stain her cheeks. "Shame on you, Jim!" she admon-
ished. "You shouldn't be looking at the ladies. Not
a happily married old man like you!"

They had developed an easy camaraderie over the

past two months, particularly after the wild ride into Middlesboro the night Cassie had given birth. The way Jim drove, Gin had been certain she would crash on the steep roads; afterward she had confided her fears to him. Ever since then he had teased her unmercifully about her driving habits, while she had teased him about his casual flirting.

Jim chuckled and picked up the white letters he had been placing on the wall directory and rolled them around in his calloused hand. "Cain't unnerstand why a good-looker like you ain't hitched," he said, purposely emphasizing the mountain twang. "Ain't natcherl, a woman like you bein' alone. If I was Dr. Douglas, I'd have ya warmin' my bed at night."

"Jim!" Gin gasped. "I'm going to tell Cassie to hit you over the head with her frying pan the next time I visit!" Gin's eyes were wide with surprise. "Dr. Douglas and I are just good friends!"

"Maybe he's cagier than either of us think." Jim continued to smile at her, obviously pleased with the effect his words had had on her. Jim always said he liked to shock her just to watch her turn what he called a bright shade of red that rivaled the fires of hell.

"Well, he'd best keep you a little busier. I can see you've got too much time on your hands, Jim Laughton!" Gin said in mock outrage.

"With all the new docs flyin' in, I'm as busy as a hog sloppin' in mud," Jim said, crooking his head toward the new wing of offices. "That one whut arrived today shure is good-lookin' Miz Gin. They be a man whut would heat up any woman's heart as well as her thighs. I'd be willin' to bet they's gonna be lots of women from the Heights gettin' headaches, and he'd better be ready to reckon with their ailments." He shrugged his shoulders expressively. "With a given name right from the Bible, I guess God saw fit to give the handsome devil a cross to bear."

It took Gin a few moments to absorb what Jim had said, but when his meaning sank in, she felt as if someone had punched her in the stomach. She placed a trembling hand on his arm. "What—what did you say? W-what's his name?" she asked, feeling her heart skip a few beats.

"Why, Noah," Jim said, looking at her with concern. "Noah Grady."

Jim rambled on about arks and animals, but Gin hardly heard a word. She stalked down the hall until she found the door bearing Noah's name. Ironically, it was across from her own office. How she had missed the large, wooden sign these past few days was beyond her. She opened the door without knocking, and an icy rage swept over her when she saw him standing nonchalantly behind his desk. "What the hell do you think you're doing?" she demanded, slamming the door shut behind her.

Noah smiled politely. "Thanks for the warm welcome. I think it's called hanging out my shingle," he said, folding his arms across his chest and appraising her boldly.

Gin scanned the back wall of his office, which was already littered with numerous diplomas and certificates. A huge sign that stood out from the rest caught her attention. Engraved in letters at least three inches tall, it proclaimed: "Chickens Accepted in lieu of Cash."

"I don't believe you have the gall to do this, Noah," she said, riveting her gaze on the proud thrust of his jaw.

"What? Hang up the sign or become a partner in Whitney Clinic?" he asked. "Two months ago you accused me of being greedy. Douglas made me an offer, and I decided it was too good to turn down, so here I am, comfortably ensconced in the hills of Kentuck." He slurred the last three words of his sentence in imitation of a Southern accent.

"I'm a partner here, too," Gin snapped. "We'll just see about that."

"Junior partner," Noah corrected. "It might interest you to know that you're now snarling at your new boss, Miss Selton."

"Why are you doing this to me?" Gin nearly shouted. Why, oh why couldn't she control her temper around him, she asked herself for the thousandth time.

"And what *am* I doing to you?" Noah asked, his tone patient and tolerant.

"If you think you can seduce me—" Gin began, but clamped her lips tight as Noah rounded the desk and strode over to her.

"I'm capable of controlling my baser instincts, Miss Selton. Are you?" He captured her hands behind her back and held his lips against hers in what seemed an endless kiss.

Gin tried to resist, but she hardly realized when her struggles ceased and her response began. Her body swayed toward his, her heart thumping erratically, and she arched against him. Laughing softly, Noah pushed her away and shrugged, his eyes mocking. "You see," he said without a trace of passion. "No untoward effects."

Deeply disturbed by his kiss and her own burning response to it, Gin was trembling almost uncontrollably. Aside from a few ragged breaths, Noah seemed as composed as he had been before. He turned away and sat back down at his desk. "Good day, Miss Selton," he said, dismissing her.

Anger so intense that it almost choked her swept through Gin, draining the blood from her face. She whirled out of the room, slamming the door shut as hard as she could, then marched into Douglas Whitney's office, again without knocking.

Some time later she closed the door softly behind her, although she was still seething with rage. Douglas had confirmed Noah's claims, pointing out to Gin all the advantages of attracting someone of Noah Grady's stature to this clinic.

Gin had hardly listened as he rattled off figures and sources of income. She was only aware of one thing— Noah Grady was back in her life, and there wasn't a damned thing she could do about it!

Gin almost declined when Douglas offered to take her to dinner later that night, but at the last moment she decided that his company might improve her disposition. She had been irritable all day, snapping mercilessly at Jim and making a total chaos of her files. She had decided to reorganize her entire office and had been shoving furniture around for quite some time. She had been just about ready to drop from fatigue when Douglas had tapped softly on her door.

He started to mumble a sheepish apology for not informing her of Noah's move, but Gin refused to listen to any explanations, brushing his words aside with a wave of her hand. She was too tired to argue with him.

As they walked to the café it dawned on Gin that one of the main reasons she was going out to dinner with Douglas was to avoid going back to her apartment, where she was sure Noah was waiting for her. He knew of her weakness where he was concerned, even if he didn't realize that she loved him, and he knew she would be unable to resist the attraction that existed between them. She was certain he planned to seduce her at the earliest opportunity—and that she would eventually give in to him.

Gin was studying the menu intently. All at once a tall male body slid into the booth beside Douglas. She looked up in stunned surprise. Noah nodded politely at her, his gray eyes sparkling with an emotion she couldn't read.

Gin slammed the menu down on the table and rose to leave, but she was jerked back by Douglas's hand on her arm. "Sit down, Gin," he commanded. "If we're going to be working together, we have to get along."

Gin clenched her jaw to keep from uttering a sarcastic retort and glared daggers at Noah from across the table. The waitress had to ask her what she wanted twice before Gin was able to stammer her order. When it was Noah's turn, he looked at her, a smile tugging at his lips. "Chicken," he told the waitress. "Miss Selton highly recommends it." For Gin's ears alone he added, "And since I may be getting paid in chickens, I'd better learn to like it."

When the waitress left, Gin glared at Douglas. "Did you plan this?" she demanded in her haughtiest voice.

"I think there's a lot we have to discuss, Gin. I want my clinic to flow smoothly during this phase of expansion. You know I intend to break ground soon for the new hospital. Surely you and Dr. Grady can put your personal problems aside for the sake of our patients."

Gin clamped her lips into a tight line and nodded in agreement. She felt even more ridiculous than she had a few moments ago, and it embarrassed her to think that Douglas had reprimanded her. When her meal arrived, she ate in silence, forcing the food down her throat without tasting a bite. She concentrated on listening to Noah and Douglas discuss their plans, trying vainly to understand the complicated financial estimates.

Noah ate with his usual hearty appetite, offering several compliments about the greens and staring at Gin as if she were responsible for cooking them. Then he bent to study the blueprints Douglas had spread out on the table.

Several hours later Douglas rolled the plans into a neat bundle and excused himself to return to the clinic. Gin rose also, but stopped abruptly when Noah rested his hand on her arm.

"If we intend to get through this transition smoothly," he said, his voice devoid of emotion, "there are a few things we need to clarify, Miss Selton. We can either discuss them here or in your apartment, whichever you prefer."

"You're mistaken, Grady, if you think I'm going to fall into bed with you again," Gin said to him after Douglas had left. "That's why you're doing this, isn't it?"

"That's quite a compliment you just gave yourself," Noah said. He sipped his coffee and stretched his limbs casually, leaning back in the booth. "If I remember my human anatomy and physiology correctly, you're not built much differently from any other woman." He raked his eyes over her, taking in her lifeless hair, lackluster complexion, and gaunt cheeks. "I'm not *that* enamored of your lovemaking to chase across the country for it. I hate to disappoint you, Miss Selton, but you had absolutely nothing to do with my decision to practice medicine here."

"Then why are you here?" Gin asked, uncertain of his real motives.

"That's a complicated question. Suffice it to say that aside from the challenge and, of course, the money, I'm interested in the welfare of my child— which you happen to be carrying. When I was here two weeks ago, you weren't taking its health and well-being into careful consideration. You still look as if you're deathly ill. I intend to make sure this baby has my watchful protection as well as my name."

"I see," Gin said, folding her hands beneath her

chin in what she hoped was a pensive pose. "Aside from the fact that my health is really none of your business, I fail to see how you're going to accomplish all this, since I've already declined your offer of marriage."

Noah smiled patiently at her. "I've already started the proper legal proceedings to declare myself the father of this child. Unless you wish to have your name dragged through various courts, I suggest you cooperate fully. I'm no longer offering to marry you. Leprosy remains a dread and puzzling disease. I checked—even marriage isn't a cure."

Gin blinked in amazement. He sounded dead serious. "W-when did this child start meaning so much to you?"

"The moment I learned of its conception," he said. "Strangely enough, fatherhood appeals to me, although I doubt if you'll choose to believe that. It might be my Italian heritage—a son to carry on the name and all that." He shrugged. "I want this child very much, and I'm extremely disturbed by its mother's state of health." He pointed to her glass of milk. "Drink up."

It was hard for Gin to defy him when his expression remained merely concerned. She didn't quite know how to categorize the man sitting across from her. His new and strange attitude confused her. He wasn't being exactly arrogant, but he *was* domineering. And it was also clear he intended to be a father to their child whether she liked it or not.

"I will admit, Noah, that my knowledge of obstetrics is still somewhat limited, but it's my understanding that expectant mothers should remain calm. Anger isn't good for a developing fetus. I shouldn't have to remind you what our past relationship has been like."

"I don't think that presents any problem, Gin." She

glanced up at his use of her first name, realizing that this was the first time he had used it. Coming from him it sounded cold and for some reason it bothered her more than when he called her Miss Selton.

Noah smiled almost as if he could read her thoughts, then continued. "I will not bother you except to inquire about your advancing pregnancy or to remind you occasionally of your limitations if I feel you're attempting anything that might harm the fetus. But other than that there should be no reason for us to argue—or to see each other, for that matter, since that's the way you want it. We may have a rare mutual patient, but since my field is neurosurgery and yours is family medicine, we probably won't have much professional contact.

"Based on our past . . . relationship . . . I find it hard to believe you don't intend to . . . seduce me," Gin said haltingly, unable to prevent a warm flush from sweeping over her face and throat. She knew she sounded as if she were inviting him into her bed.

Noah looked at her for a long moment. "I didn't mean to give you the impression that your body is repulsive," he said, flashing a wry grin. "If you should decide to stop playing silly games, come see me. Perhaps we can work out something agreeable. But until you wish it otherwise, our relationship needn't be other than strictly professional. If that should change, you'll have to come to me this time."

For a moment Gin found it difficult to understand him. Noah had as much as told her he wasn't interested in her, even sexually, and as incongruous as it seemed, *that* confused her. Although she wanted to deny it, she had to face the fact that she was still attracted to him, that his presence was very disturbing. Intellectually she knew he was appealing to basic human nature: you don't realize how much you want something until it's taken away. He hadn't totally fooled her. He had thrown the gauntlet down, but she wasn't about to pick it up and fall into his trap.

"All right, Noah," she said. "I think you may be right. We should be able to work together amicably if we both try, but I'll warn you only once. If you so much as come near my apartment or try to make love to me, I'll leave Sandy Point and you will never, *ever* see this child." Although Gin spoke softly, there was a harsh tone to her voice that left no doubt of her sincerity.

Noah finished his coffee and rose, holding out his hand to help her from the booth. Without speaking they walked to the clinic parking lot where he helped her into her Jeep. Noah jumped into the silver Mercedes and sped into the dark Appalachian night.

Gin sat in the Jeep for a few moments without turning the ignition key, listening to the soft evening noises. Crickets were chirping in a nearby gully, and from behind the building an owl hooted, his mournful tune an eerie echo. Gin sighed and started the motor.

For the next several days their relationship remained strictly professional. Noah asked Gin several times a day how she felt—if she was eating properly and if she was resting. Other than that he barely glanced at her. Their conversation was limited to what was required for the smooth functioning of Whitney Clinic.

Gin admitted she was slightly hurt that he seemed no longer interested in her, that the physical attraction between them was something only she continued to feel. It was difficult to look seductive in a nurse's uniform, and she wouldn't have tried anyhow, but she began to take a new interest in her appearance—making an effort to have her hair styled and wearing lipstick whenever she was at the clinic. But as the days progressed, Gin found that the continuous stream of wealthy, attractive female patients Noah had already attracted made him less accessible to her.

A few days later she remarked to Douglas that if the present flow of patients continued, Noah would be able to build the hospital on his fees alone. Douglas stared dumfounded at her, then shook his head and sighed, muttering an unintelligible comment about women. Realizing that she must have sounded jealous, Gin excused herself and closed her office door, throwing herself into her work.

She held off as long as she could, but later that day she admitted she had to visit Noah. She needed his opinion. She rapped on his door and entered before she could change her mind.

"Good afternoon, Miss Selton," Noah said, rising from his chair. He poured two cups of coffee from the percolator he always kept going and handed her a cup.

"You're going to develop pancreatic problems, Grady," she told him. "You drink too much coffee."

He cocked a dark eyebrow at her. "I'm surprised you care, Miss Selton. Is that your way of expressing an interest in resuming our relationship?"

She glared at him. "I was merely making an observation." she snapped.

"You have a habit of saying one thing and meaning another, Miss Selton. I just wanted to clarify your purpose."

"I'm also sorry you find my habits disturbing," she said, checking the sarcasm that had crept into her voice.

"You have a lot of disturbing qualities, Miss Selton, the least of which are your habits."

"Look, Noah, I didn't come here to spar with you. I have something important to discuss."

"Dr. Grady," he said.

"What?" she asked. She was having trouble following his typically confusing conversation.

"Since we aren't exchanging pleasantries, and our relationship is strictly professional, I suggest you call me Dr. Grady."

Gin heaved a sigh and slapped the chart she had been carrying in her hands onto his desk. "This patient is pregnant. She is also an epileptic. I'd like your opinion, *Dr. Grady*."

Noah sat down in his swivel chair and, taking the chart in his hands, leaned back to flip through her notes and the various tests she had run on the patient. After several minutes he looked back up at her. "Your treatment is fine. I don't have any further suggestions. Test her blood for therapeutic-drug levels every two months and check her more frequently than you otherwise would. Other than that, she should be controlled enough to withstand childbirth. Would you like me to examine her?"

"Only if she should develop complications," Gin said, taking the chart from him. She rose to leave. "Thank you," she said politely.

"Wait, Ginny," Noah said when she started to open the door.

"Miss Selton," she corrected, pausing for effect.

"All right, point taken," Noah said with a sheepish look. "Can we talk?"

"Is it personal or professional?" Gin couldn't help asking.

"Personal." Noah leaned back in his chair and crossed his hands behind his head, his gaze fixed on the swell of her breasts in what could only be termed a hungry look.

Gin shivered and opened the door. "Then no," she said, closing it behind her with a firm click.

She leaned against the door and let out a long, slow breath, closing her eyes. When she reopened them, Douglas was standing beside her.

"Consultation?" he asked, his face kind and concerned.

"Castigation," Gin amended pushing away from the door and walking back to her office.

The polite pattern of their days continued for the next week, except that Gin avoided Noah as much as possible, the strain of their relationship beginning to wear on her nerves. Even though the nausea had subsided, she was still fatigued, and she spent every evening at home waiting anxiously for him to knock at her door. So far he'd been true to his word and hadn't approached her.

One weekday she sat at her desk, tapping a pencil on the smooth surface, and looked out at a mockingbird that had made the sycamore outside her window its home. For some reason she was irritated at the bright spring day—and with Noah's indifference, she admitted, tapping the pencil harder and watching the bird wriggle into its nest. What had Noah said in the restaurant the day he'd returned? This time, you'll have to come see me. Gin clutched the pencil harder. Did she want this relationship regardless of his feelings? She finally asked herself. He'd proven he wanted their child; he was willing to assume the responsibility of a family. Unable to face the answers just yet, Gin threw the pencil aside, picked up the chart she'd been studying, and walked across the hall.

"Good morning." Noah looked surprised when he answered her knock. He glanced at the chart in her hands. "Another mutual patient?" he asked with a grin. "It's amazing how many pregnant women here have neurological problems."

"Can't we just drop the nonsense, Grady?" He was always purposely goading her.

Noah sat down on the edge of the desk and indicated a nearby chair. "The only nonsense I'm aware of is our whole relationship. It's a sham," he said, arching an eyebrow at her. "But it needn't be, since it's obvious we both want the same thing."

Gin grasped the chart tightly, her knuckles turning white. *Why* did he have to irritate her? "Moving here hasn't improved you one bit, Grady!" she snapped when she could speak again. "You're still arrogant and insensitive." She slammed the chart down on his desk. "Let me know what you think by interoffice memo. Perhaps we should use that means of communication in the future for anything we wish to say to each other." She left, slamming the door. His soft chuckle echoed down the hallway.

Later that night, when Gin pulled into the parking space in front of her apartment, she was surprised to see Noah waiting in his car. Their encounter that morning hadn't been very pleasant, and she was astonished that he would come to her after all.

She shut off the Jeep and swung out of it, trying to fight a weakness that made her limbs refuse to function, and walked toward the Mercedes. She hadn't the vaguest idea what she was going to say. She only knew his presence made her pulses quicken even though he continued to irritate her.

Noah got out from behind the wheel of the sleek car and held up a huge brown bag. "I brought supper," he said with a lopsided grin. "You looked tired today. I thought you might appreciate not having to cook." He leaned casually on the car door. "I didn't think it would be quite the same via interoffice memo."

Gin ignored his comment and glanced at the bag. She would have known instinctively what it contained even if she hadn't been able to smell the mouth-watering aroma of fried chicken.

"When are you going to stop this charade, Grady?" she asked, trying to feign a casualness she didn't feel.

He pretended to be crushed. "I've developed a

fondness for chicken," he said, shaking his head at her. "How could you make such an accusation?" He stared at her with a mournful expression.

"Past experience," she commented with an offhand shrug. "Has anyone paid you with poultry yet?"

"Just yesterday a patient gave me a dozen eggs." He grinned, shifting the bag in his hands. "Well," he said after the silence had stretched interminably between them, "shall we go up and eat? The peace offering is getting cold."

Gin bristled. He just *assumed* they would fall into the same pattern as they had in Minnesota. "Have you forgotten my warning, Noah?" she asked, leaning against his shiny car. "I told you never to come to my apartment."

"I'm aware of your threat," he said, still grinning.

"I mean it, Grady!"

"Are you afraid of me?" he asked, his eyebrow cocked, "or of yourself?"

Because the astuteness of his question made her uncomfortable, Gin snapped at him. "Take that stupid chicken and go home, Grady!"

He chuckled and placed a hand on the roof of the car just inches from her shoulder. "You must be Irish, Ginny. You have a terrible temper and a very short fuse."

Gin pushed herself away from the car and started to stalk off, but he reached out and grabbed her arm. "I'm sorry, Ginny," he said. "I only meant to express my concern for your health. If you really don't want to go to your apartment, there's a roadside picnic area a couple miles from here. We can go there. I wouldn't dare touch you in the presence of other people." He held up the bag of chicken. "It would be a shame to waste good food."

Gin wasn't sure if it was his appeal to her practical nature or her sudden desire to be with him that convinced her, but she nodded meekly, then let him usher her into the Mercedes. Relaxing against the plush upholstered seat, she stared out the window at the scenery whizzing by as he guided the car expertly along the curving highway. In contrast to the Jeep, which jostled and bounced with a loud roar, the car hugged the road smoothly, its engine a low whine.

When they pulled into the graveled rest area, Gin surveyed the huge, gnarled trees, the dense, budding foliage, and the empty tables, then glared at Noah.

He shrugged and got out to open her door. "I thought it would be crowded," he explained, flashing her another grin. "It's a lovely night for a picnic."

"And it's also too far to walk home," she retorted.

"Ginny," he said impatiently, "if you thought it would irritate me, you're stubborn enough to try it."

Gin ignored his comment, realizing there was some truth to his words, and spread out their dinner. Noah pulled a bottle of white wine from another paper bag and unscrewed the cork, then handed her a cupful.

"Is this to make me languid and responsive to your embrace?" she asked, immediately wanting to bite her tongue. Would she never learn to keep her mouth shut?

"You needn't worry about having to endure my caresses, Ginny," Noah said with a trace of bitterness. "There are numerous women around here who are willing to satisfy my...needs. I've never forced myself on one yet, and I don't intend to start now. I've told you several times that I'm only concerned about the child."

Gin lowered her eyes to avoid meeting his, certain he could see how desperately she wanted him to take her in his arms and crush her to his body. To cover her acute embarrassment, she picked up a chicken leg and started to nibble at the crisp crust.

Dusk had fallen by the time they finished eating,

and tiny fireflies were flitting about, their luminescence flickering in the deepening night. Gin remembered making rings and bracelets from their bodies as a child and wondered now how she could have cruelly plucked them apart. She watched them fly aimlessly, shivering involuntarily when the breeze grew cool.

"Cold?" Noah asked, tucking his suit jacket around her shoulders. "We can go back."

Gin shook her head. "I love the nights here. I could listen to the sounds forever. It's so different from everywhere else I've lived." She scanned the rambling terrain.

"It's a little like the chicken, isn't it?" Noah said in response. "It grows on you gradually."

Gin nodded, wondering if her pensive mood was a result of the glass of wine she had consumed or if she was experiencing another of the hormonal imbalances that had begun to bother her. She sighed and stared into the night.

"Are you all right, Ginny?" Noah asked, concerned.

She turned to him but couldn't see his face, which was hidden in the darkness. This was a new, gentler Noah, and it intrigued her. "Yes," she said. "I'm fine."

"I thought we could talk now," he continued, his voice low and husky.

Gin cleared her throat, trying to shake the mood that had gripped her. She felt as if she was going to burst into tears at any moment. "Ply me with food and wine, then invite me into your web," she said, half joking. Like the spider to the fly, she thought. "Are you going to ask me to marry you again, or do you intend to simply seduce me?" Her voice sounded harsh, even to her, in her attempt to hide a sudden surge of melancholy.

"You made it clear before that you're not interested in marrying me. Have you changed your mind?"

"Not without love," she said. Fool that I am, she wanted to add, but turned away from him. "I'm not interested in a relationship based on mere desire," she whispered. Not that her protest would do much good, she sighed to herself. If he so much as touched her now, she would probably fall into his arms.

She was standing beside the picnic table and could feel him move up behind her. "Is it mere desire to want to touch you?" he asked, nearly whispering. "To hold you, to feel you beneath my body? Is it mere desire to want to protect you, to walk beside you and be with you?" He was so close she could feel his soft breath on the back of her neck, and she shivered again, while a hot, burning flush spread up her body and into her face. She waited for him to take her in his arms.

He was standing behind her, and she felt him hesitate, sensed him lift his arms and then let them fall to his sides. She stood utterly still, waiting for him to make up his mind, her thoughts a jumble of half-formed fears and expectations.

Gin tried to swallow the lump that had formed in her throat. "I...I..." She started to say, "I love you," but the words died in her throat as the damp night air crawled up her spine. Noah had turned abruptly away, and the coldness of his rejection replaced the flush in her cheeks with an icy tingle.

As she watched him clear away the remains of their dinner, she wondered what had happened to break the magic spell that had enclosed them for a few moments.

"Noah?" She started to ask him what was wrong, but he glanced at her with a brief flicker of his eyes that was so forbidding that she trembled again. This time it wasn't from desire.

"I'll take you home, Ginny," he said gruffly when

he had disposed of the last of the trash. He headed toward the car without a backward glance.

As he drove back toward town, Gin fixed her eyes on the yellow ribbon that divided the road, occasionally stealing glances at his set profile, which was outlined by the headlights of passing cars. She yearned for the closeness they had once shared. She loved him. She would never stop loving him, and now she regretted having turned down his offers of marriage, no matter how they had been proffered.

Minutes later he pulled up in front of her apartment house and screeched to a halt. Without looking at her, he leaned over and opened the car door. "See you tomorrow, Miss Selton," he said as she got out, and roared away.

chapter 12

B<small>UT</small> G<small>IN</small> didn't see him the next day. The shivering and hot, burning feeling she'd had during dinner that evening must have been influenza, she realized as she snuggled under the blankets that night, shaking uncontrollably. She sipped hot tea with lemon and blew her nose incessantly. Doctors and nurses weren't supposed to get sick, she thought as she flicked out the lamp at her bedside.

The next morning she called Douglas. At the sound of her hoarse voice, he issued a stern reprimand and ordered her to remain in bed for the day.

Taking her tissues and a jug of juice to the bedroom, Gin gladly followed his advice, feeling more miserable than she had in months.

Gin finally opened her eyes and realized that the pounding and shouting weren't part of her dream. They came from outside her front door. The red dials of her clock read 2:00 A.M. She sat up, shaking her head to dispel her grogginess. The textbook she had

161

been reading before she'd drifted off to sleep fell to the floor. Finally recognizing Noah's voice, she groped for her robe, wrapped the pale, diaphanous fabric around her body, and stumbled to the door.

Noah was still pounding and ringing the buzzer, shouting her name over and over. Gin flipped the lock and opened the door, wiping sleep from her eyes. "What's wrong, Noah?" she asked, fighting a lingering languor.

"Are you all right, Ginny?" he asked, relief flooding his voice.

"I'm fine. Why?" She realized that he was still standing outside, and she motioned for him to enter.

"Douglas mentioned earlier that you weren't feeling well. I drove by on my way from Middlesboro to check you, and when I saw your light burning, I thought something had happened to you."

Gin closed the door behind him. "I have a cold and was studying for an exam. I guess I must have fallen asleep." She looked up at him. "My apartment is out of your way, Noah. You didn't have to drive by," she said, feeling suddenly soft and vulnerable as she stared up into his eyes.

"I check every night, Ginny." Noah's voice was husky with emotion.

Gin reached out to brush a stray lock of dark hair from his forehead, the gesture so natural it didn't occur to her to check it. She noticed the tiny lines around his sensitive lips. "You look tired, Noah."

"Sometimes I think there are more gruesome car accidents on these roads than there are in the entire state of Minnesota," he said, reaching up to catch her hand in his and squeezing tightly. "I lost a patient tonight, although I worked very hard to save him. His wife is still critical."

Gin searched his face, touched at the stark pain that shone from his gray eyes, and reached out again to smooth the worry from his forehead. She stood on tiptoe and fluttered her fingers over his mouth, wanting to comfort him and yearning to feel his lips possess hers.

He stared back at her, his eyes dark with passion. She drew the flimsy material of her robe tighter around her in an involuntary gesture of shyness, suddenly aware that the light from her bedroom shone through the transparent fabric, outlining the soft curves of her body. Noah's gaze followed her gesture, then traveled further, easily penetrating the gauzy gown. Her breath caught in her throat when she realized that he was staring hungrily at her body.

"I . . . I . . . Noah, you should . . ." she whispered in her confusion, not really knowing what to say, only aware of the intensity of her yearning to feel his body against hers, to feel his hands caress her feverish skin, to feel his lips claim and sear hers.

Noah ran his fingers lightly down the length of her arm and looked at her expectantly. His breathing was short and ragged. "Ginny?" he said in a hoarse plea.

Gin listened to the erratic thumping of her heart and shivered in anticipation. Hardly conscious of her actions, she closed the distance that separated them, reaching her hands up to circle his neck. Twining her fingers in his dark hair, she pulled his head down to meet her waiting lips.

Noah kissed her hungrily, greedily drinking in her mouth, her throat, the feel and touch of her, exploring her lips with his moist tongue as his hands sought and found her ripe breasts, made fuller by the child nestled within her.

With a tiny cry of gladness, Gin arched her body against the full length of his, lost in the sensations of their embrace. She drew her hands over his arms, then moved them along the tight, corded muscles of his back, stretched taut as he held her, finally coming around to his chest, where she buried her fingers in the hair that protruded from his unbuttoned shirt.

"Oh, God, Ginny," he breathed. "I want you. Please love me," he whispered, cupping a breast in his hand and teasing the nipple erect with his fingertip.

"I love you, Noah," she whispered back. "Make love to me . . . oh, please, now."

Noah groaned and swept her up in his arms, his lips still clinging to hers, and brought her into the bedroom, laying her tenderly on the silky sheets of her bed. Opening her robe, he slid it over her shoulders, his lips trailing sensuously over her creamy skin. With another groan, he buried his face in the hollow of her breasts, then rolled her on top of him, peeling her gown off and running his lips and tongue over her bare breasts. Gin gasped when he cupped both breasts, thrusting them upward with his hands and teasing the nipples with tiny nips of his teeth. "Ginny, Ginny, my love," he whispered against the curve of her throat.

She looked down at him, love shining from her blue eyes, and slowly, agonizingly, she unbuttoned his shirt, running her hands over his chest and along his arms as she stripped him of his clothes.

Gin wasn't aware of the exact moment when she ceased to think rational thoughts, she was so swept up in the wild, sweet force of their passion. She only knew she responded eagerly to his caresses, matching each with one of her own, letting him know with her touch how deeply she loved him.

When Noah possessed her, making her think she would explode from the intense shuddering of her body, it was the most bittersweet moment of her life. She was lifted and sent soaring to the precipice of fulfillment. Thousands of tiny stars shattered around her, and the world whirled with dizzying force as Noah stroked her to a quivering peak, then brought her over the tumult of pleasure into a sea of tranquility.

Tears of joy slipped from her closed eyes. The incredible beauty of her love had transformed the union of their bodies into an expression of deep and abiding significance.

The last thing Gin remembered before drifting into a contented sleep was being wrapped in the protective circle of Noah's arms and snuggling against his chest. She woke several hours later to a cold, empty bed and looked frantically around the room, fearful that he had gone. She sighed with relief when she saw him standing by the window, his lean, muscular body visible in the gray light of dawn.

"Noah?" she called softly.

He turned and walked back to the bed, but in the shadowy room Gin couldn't see his face clearly. "Go back to sleep, Ginny," he said, reaching to pull a stray lock of hair from her face.

When Gin woke again much later, bright sunshine was streaming into the room, bathing her in a warm glow that matched the tender rush of love she felt when her eyes found him. Noah was fully dressed in a dark suit that fit his frame snugly. He was standing beside the bed staring down at her.

Looking up into his face, Gin felt tears slipping down her cheeks. The recollection of her total surrender to him streamed into her mind, and she averted her eyes, struggling to hide the warm flush that was spreading across her body. She squirmed under the sheet, embarrassed by her ridiculous reaction, knowing that the hormonal changes she was undergoing as well as the intensity of her feelings for him were making her teary-eyed.

"You have to believe I never meant for this to happen," Noah finally said, shoving his hands deep into his pockets. His voice sounded tortured, and for a moment she thought he was going to beg her forgiveness. "I swear I'll never touch you again," he continued, running his hand through his hair, his unconscious gesture tugging at her heart. He hesitated, then turned to leave.

"Noah, wait!" Gin called when he started for the door. She sprang from the bed. Realizing she was still naked when the cold air hit her skin, she searched the rumpled covers for her gown and, finally retrieving it, she tried to shove her arms into the twisted material before he could leave. "Noah, we have to talk!" she cried, running into the living room after him.

Noah paused at the door and turned to her again, then reached to flick the switch of his pocket pager to still the shrill beeping. "I have to go to Middlesboro, Ginny. Promise me you won't do anything foolish until I get back." He caressed her cheek briefly and left before she could say anything.

Gin gaped at the closed door, all of a sudden aware that he thought she was upset about what had happened between them. Didn't he realize she had wanted it as much as he? Hadn't he heard her declaration of love last night? Why did her angry words always return to haunt her?

She leaned against the wall, her thoughts in turmoil. Oh, Noah, you silly, beautiful man, she lamented to herself. Didn't he know she loved him and could never leave him now? If only you loved me, she thought, then realized that, regardless of his feelings, she had accepted the consequences of loving a man without demanding anything in return—come what may.

Gin twisted her hair into a snug knot at the nape of her neck. Her morning at the clinic had been terribly busy, and she was going to be late for her classes if she didn't leave soon. She jabbed a final pin into her hair and picked up her books, sighing and checking her watch. The jangling telephone interrupted her departure.

"Miz Gin," Darlene, the clerk at Whitney Clinic, said when Gin answered. "Jim Laughton's lookin' for you. He says they need you right away out at the house. Do you suppose it's the baby. They just brought him home yesterday."

"I don't know, Darlene. Didn't you ask what the problem was?"

"No. Jim was really upset and said he needed you as soon as possible. Can you go?"

"Of course. I'll leave now," Gin said. "Has Dr. Grady returned from Middlesboro yet?" she asked, then realized Darlene had already broken the connection.

Gin searched for a pen and paper. The last time she had gone somewhere, Noah had been upset because she hadn't left him a note. The night she'd spent with Suzanne he'd been furious. He would be anxious about her now, she realized. He had left that morning without knowing she loved him, and she didn't want him to worry when he returned and found her gone.

She scrawled a quick explanation on a piece of paper, then reread the message: "Noah—Had to leave before you returned." She wanted to add, "I love you," but since she planned to leave the note on her front door, she smiled to herself and added instead: "Found a cure for leprosy. Ginny." She wished she had time to write more, but the urgency of Jim's call worried her, and besides, Noah would understand what she meant. She loved him and was ready and willing to marry him!

She stuck the note on her front door with a thumbtack and ran to her Jeep, shoving it into gear almost before the motor caught.

Gin bumped along the roads, twisting the wheel to avoid the sucking mud puddles in the unpaved lanes. She ignored the lump in her throat and refused to look at the sheer drop on the passenger side of the Jeep, wondering if she would ever conquer her fear of driving in these mountains. As she approached the rambling buildings of the Laughton farm, she grew more and more anxious. Jim would call only if he was desperate.

When she walked in the front door, Gin quickly assessed the situation and set her nurse's bag aside. She wanted to laugh with blessed relief. Cassie Laughton was sobbing, and the baby that was trying to nuzzle at her breast was alternately squalling and stiffening his body. Jim Laughton was pacing the floor, trying vainly to comfort the two towheaded little girls who were clinging to him and also crying. Clothes were strewn all over the place, dirty dishes and toys littered the room, and it was obvious that the entire family hadn't slept all night.

"Miz Gin," Cassie wailed. "I don't seem to have any milk. The baby must be sick. He's cried all night. I was so scared to bring him home. The doctors said he still needed a lot of care but we wanted him with us."

Gin sent Jim to the Jeep for a box of supplies she always kept in the back, then took the baby from Cassie's arms. He turned and nuzzled, seeking hungrily, and when his efforts were frustrated turned red and screamed with wrath.

Cassie sat in a rocking chair, her face anxious, and burst into a fresh squall of tears when the child screamed. "I cain't lose him," she whispered. "Oh, what am I gonna do?"

"Jim." Gin turned to him as soon as he returned, making her voice stern and authoritative. "You take Cassie into the bathroom and make sure she takes a long, leisurely bath. Here." She grabbed a bar of lavender-scented soap from the box he'd brought in and tossed it toward him. "There's nothing wrong with this child. All of you are overreacting to the situation, and I want you to listen carefully." She turned to Cassie. "The baby is fine, but you're a nervous wreck. Jim, I want you to stay with Cassie and scrub her back. Put her to bed and make certain she's relaxed and sleeping. Don't leave until she is. I'll take care of everything here."

Cassie cast her a weary, relieved look and followed Jim into the bathroom. Calling to the two children to follow her, Gin reached in the box for a bottle of formula and dragged the rickety rocking chair into the kitchen. It was her favorite room in the Laughton home, huge and warm, with shiny wood cabinets that smelled pleasantly and a delightful view of the mountains from the back door.

Gin handed the children a box of crayons and two huge coloring books, laughing when their tears dried up magically. As they sat on the floor beside her filling in the pages, Gin, relaxing in the chair, fed the baby, rocking to and fro while he sucked greedily at the bottle.

Later she burped him and laid him in a nearby bassinet to sleep. She ran water in the huge kitchen sink, then stripped the girls, scrubbing them until their skins glowed pink and they were giggling with glee and slapping at the soap bubbles. When she had finished bathing them she dressed them in jerseys and overalls, then lit the ancient gas stove and scrambled some eggs.

She watched the children eat, their natural exuberance contagious as they shoveled food into their mouths. Then she gathered up the laundry and washed the dishes, glancing from time to time at the peaceful infant. He was squirming but still asleep. The girls became absorbed in some toys and Gin was searching in the cabinet for detergent to wash the clothes when Jim Laughton entered the room.

"Well, that took you long enough! What-all did you wash?" Gin said, then laughed when Jim blushed a bright red.

"You said . . ." Jim turned an even darker shade of red and squirmed uncomfortably, then mumbled, "She's asleep."

"I'll bet she is!" Gin teased again. "Talk about rivaling the fires of hell, Jim Laughton. You should see your face!"

"Miz Gin, you shore do confuse a body. You say one thing an' mean another. You tole me to make shore she was relaxed, and I done my best."

"I'm sorry, Jim," Gin said, her voice at once sober. "You're right. I did say that, and you're not the first man to tell me I'm confusing. Look, the baby is asleep, and there's absolutely nothing wrong with him or with Cassie."

"But what about her milk?" Jim asked. "She had plenty for the other young uns, and she's been pumpin' it like you said and sendin' it to Middlesboro. Delores Flemming said it must have soured and the baby'd be poisoned 'cause Cassie done somethin' the Lord didn't like."

"That's superstitious nonsense, Jim!" Gin said. "Cassie is very anxious about this baby. She almost lost her life when she delivered him, and then she almost lost him. He's been a little spoiled by the hospital nurses and will be more demanding for a few weeks. Cassie's so afraid she's going to do something to harm him that she's not letting her milk down. You have to make sure she rests properly and drinks lots of fluids. Encourage her to relax and enjoy the baby."

Jim nodded his understanding and glanced at the

child, who was pursing his mouth and wriggling in the crib. "He's so durn little," he said. "An' he's still fidgety."

"He'll grow sooner than you think," Gin replied. "And he's fidgety because he swallowed a lot of air while he was crying," she explained. "He'll have some gas pains tonight, but he should be fine. I want you to bring them both to the clinic tomorrow. We'll have the new pediatrician examine him, and I'd like Dr. Douglas to see Cassie just to reassure her. You're to take the next week off with pay and help out around here. Okay?"

Jim looked at her anxiously. "We got a lotta bills over at the hospital. I don't rightly reckon Doc Douglas is gonna give me time off with pay, even iffen you tell him."

Gin arched an eyebrow at him, but other than that she let the comment pass. Jim Laughton probably had never heard of the women's movement. "I'm one of the bosses," she explained. "But if it will make you feel any better, I'll stop and talk to Dr. Douglas on my way home. He might have some ideas about what we can do about the hospital bills, too."

"I ain't takin' no welfare," Jim objected.

"No, Jim, I didn't imagine you would." Gin turned to the washing machine. "How does this thing work?" she asked, staring in perplexity at the strange contraption. "I don't believe I've ever seen a wringer before."

By the time Gin left the farm, she was surprised that dusk had already fallen. She hadn't realized it was so late. Flipping on the headlights of the Jeep, she fixed her eyes on the muddy road. She hated navigating it in daylight, and now that it was rapidly growing dark she would be forced to creep along until she got to town. Hitting a bone-jarring pothole, Gin braked, her palms growing sweaty.

It took Gin another hour to traverse the roads. By the time she pulled up in front of Douglas Whitney's modest frame house, she was drained of energy. She stepped down from the Jeep, thinking she should go directly home to wait for Noah, but she had promised Jim she would stop by and speak to Douglas first. Right now she was almost grateful she had made that promise. She needed time to collect herself for the hairpin curves farther down the highway.

"Got some coffee?" Gin asked when Douglas answered the door. "These roads are going to be my Waterloo."

Douglas laughed and motioned her inside. "You need a Jeep with power steering and automatic transmission." He considered her seriously. "How's Cassie? I almost came out myself, but I figured you could handle anything that might be wrong."

Gin shook her head and flashed him a wry smile. "It was nothing. Just a little emotional upset and lots of confusion, with a little mountain superstition thrown in. Actually, the most I did was wash the clothes and do the dishes."

"Mmmm." Douglas laughed again. "All those years in college wasted. Woman's work is instinctual, isn't it?"

Gin looked at him with a tolerant smirk. "It takes more than instinct to manage a wringer washer," she said. "Unfortunately, the university I attended didn't offer courses in outmoded mechanical equipment." She followed him toward the kitchen and leaned on the counter while he made coffee. "Cassie's coming in tomorrow. I'd like you to take a look at her." Douglas nodded in agreement. Gin continued, "I promised Jim the week off with pay, but he insisted I check with you."

"That must have touched off your temper," Douglas commented, pouring her a cup of coffee.

Gin sipped the strong, hot liquid. "I was in an expansive mood today," she said at last. "I let it pass."

"If you ignored that, then the bed rest yesterday must have been beneficial." Douglas grinned at her.

She wasn't sure about the rest, but the bed had been marvelous, Gin thought, then became embarrassed when she realized she was blushing.

"I'm glad you stopped by, Gin," Douglas continued, not seeming to notice her discomfort. "I've been meaning to talk to you. I want to tell you I'm proud of the way you've handled the situation with Noah Grady. I know it must be very difficult for you." Douglas opened the door to the patio as he talked, then stood aside for Gin to pass.

She went pale at his words of praise. If Douglas only knew, she thought, what would he say? She followed him to the ornamented table, avoiding his eyes, and sat down in a wrought-iron chair. Gazing at the towering hills that jutted into the starry sky, she reveled in the soft Appalachian night.

"I dearly love it here, Douglas," she said.

Douglas nodded in silent agreement, then groaned and set down his coffee when the doorbell chimed. They had both heard the roar of a car and the screech of brakes on the gravel road, but neither had thought much of it, attributing it to a reckless driver on the steep, winding road.

"I forgot about Darlene being off," Douglas muttered, crossing the patio quickly. "I hope it's not an emergency."

Gin realized she should try to call Noah and jumped up when she recognized his voice through the open screen door. She started toward the house, anxious to see him.

"Damn it, Douglas! Do you know where Ginny

has run off to? She left me this note telling me she was leaving. I've searched all over for her." Noah was shouting as Gin passed through the kitchen. She wasn't able to hear Douglas's soft answer even though she quickened her step, and it was apparent Noah hadn't, either. He had turned away and was running his fingers impatiently through his hair and pacing the room when she reached the living room doorway.

She wondered what had upset him, then remembered the critical case he had had in Middlesboro. He had been at the hospital for more than twelve hours. Maybe he'd lost another patient.

"I haven't run off anywhere, Noah," Gin said softly. "I'm right here."

chapter 13

NOAH WHIRLED to face her, blanching visibly. He looked exhausted. His suit was creased, and his tie was hanging unknotted around his open shirt. The frown ,that marred his forehead intensified the lines of weariness in his face. He glared at her, unleashing all the cumulative frustrations of the day on her. "What the *hell* are you trying to prove by doing this to me?" He held her note in his hand.

"I'm sure you'll both excuse me," Douglas mumbled, and closed the front door tactfully behind him.

"I-I thought you would understand," she stammered.

"Understand what?" Noah shouted. "That you're running away from me again? How many times do you expect me to chase after you? Haven't you punished me enough for something I didn't do?"

"I'm not punishing you, Noah," Gin started to say, "I'm—"

"For God's sake, Ginny"—his words lashed across

hers—"why can't you accept the fact that I love you? What do I have to do to convince you?"

Gin walked toward him, thinking her heart would burst with pure joy. "Did . . . did you just say you love me?" she asked, searching his face intently.

Noah hunched his shoulders and paced the floor. "Yes, damn it! Not that it means anything to—"

"Why didn't you just say so instead of ranting and raving at me?" Gin interrupted, nearly shouting to gain his attention. She lowered her voice. "I love you, too."

"Because it wouldn't make any difference to— What?" he said, spinning around to face her.

"I love you, too," Gin repeated softly. "I told you that last night. Didn't you hear me?"

Noah looked confused for a moment, then caught her in his arms, crushing her against him. "Oh God, Ginny," he said hoarsely. "I thought you were gone, and I didn't think I could stand it. Last night—"

Gin placed her fingers over his lips, stilling his voice. "Last night was the most beautiful night of my life," she whispered, her eyes shimmering with tears.

"You weren't upset? I thought . . . I thought this morning you hated me for making love to you. I . . . Ginny, I can't even think coherently when I'm near you. I love you so much."

"Noah, don't talk." Gin wound her arms around his neck. "Just hold me and love me."

Noah held her tight, almost as if he never wanted to let her out of his arms. He kissed her over and over, and through a haze of longing Gin remembered Douglas.

"Noah," she whispered when his lips left hers momentarily. "Douglas. He's outside."

Noah drew back to stare into her eyes, then chuckled softly. "The fresh mountain air will do him a world of good," he said, leaning down to kiss her again.

"This is his home," Gin said just before Noah swooped her up in his arms and strode to the sofa.

"So it is," he said, laying her down on the soft pillows, bringing his lips down to claim hers again.

Gin laughed and pushed against his chest lightly. "Dr. Grady! Control yourself!" She stared at him, her voice growing serious. "How long have you loved me?"

"Several months now," he murmured, trying to kiss her again. "I thought you didn't want to talk."

"I changed my mind." She pushed at his chest again, then leaned her head back to look inquiringly at him. "When you asked me to marry you, both times, did you love me then?"

Noah's expression told her he would much rather engage in something other than conversation, but he groaned and sat up, pulling her across his lap. "Yes. I think I've loved you from the very first moment I saw you. I nearly bit your head off, and you were so damned mad." He grinned that special lopsided smile that made her heart do flip-flops, then kissed her again, lightly brushing his lips across hers. "I pursued you relentlessly, telling myself you didn't mean anything to me, but the night the Brandner boy died I finally admitted to myself that I loved you.

Gin frowned at him. "Why didn't you tell me?"

"For a lot of reasons. I've always been so detached, Ginny. I never had time to fall in love with a woman. I never wanted just one woman until I met you. Needing you so damned much was a strange feeling that I had to fight."

Gin nodded. "I understand. I felt much the same way myself."

"To begin with, I thought you loved another man. Remember that first night I came to your apartment?

You told me about Nick, and you looked so devastated. Then you said you'd never forget him. I suspected later that you loved me and that you were lying
to yourself, but you would never admit it. The night
we argued so bitterly over Catherine Timmits you
insisted you could never love me because of Nick."

"My angry words keep haunting me," Gin said
with deep regret, running her fingers through the dark
hair at his temples.

"I knew you'd been hurt, and I suspected you were
afraid of love. I thought that by keeping you with me
you would recognize that, but when you left I had to
believe you."

"I left Minnesota because I loved you, Noah. I
didn't want to marry you because I thought you didn't
care for me. I was so afraid you couldn't settle down
to just one woman. I thought your lifestyle and medical practice were more important to you than a
woman's love. I wanted a child..." She heard her
voice break. "I...I..."

Noah cradled her in his arms. "Considering the
way I've treated women in my past, I guess I deserved
your distrust," he said thoughtfully. "But, I think that
same spunky temperament is what attracted me to you
from the very first." He grinned and looked down into
her eyes. "You were the first woman to challenge me.
You fought for what you believed in and made me
realize the inequities of medicine. I really admired
your skills, you know."

"You did?" Gin said, smiling up at him. "You
certainly didn't act like it."

"You were a threat, and you made me feel again.
For so many years I'd channeled my emotions into
my work that I think I wanted to punish you just a
bit for making me aware of the pain of learning to feel
something deeply for another person. The night Jim

Brandner died, I came to you. I knew you would understand how I felt. I exploded when you weren't there. When I finally found you, you were so cold, but that ridiculous offer I made was in earnest. I think I would have done anything to keep you by my side. I tried to prove that by making love to you."

"I thought Mary Anne—"

"Ginny," he interrupted, "there was never anything between Mary Anne Harner and me . . . or Catherine Timmits," he added. "You believe that, don't you?"

Gin nodded. "Now I do. Your reputation was so . . . Oh, Noah, it doesn't really matter anymore. We love each other and we're together."

"Thanks to Suzanne Bonati," Noah said with a wry grin.

Gin frowned. "I must apologize to her," she whispered. "I wrote her a very nasty letter after you showed up here the first time."

"I know," Noah said. "I read it when I returned to Minnesota. She was furious with me." He laughed. "Poor Suzanne. I think I drove her crazy after you left. Then when she finally told me where you were and that you were pregnant, I must have behaved like a lunatic myself. Let's just say that the last few weeks of my residency were most unpleasant for the nurses at Lakeside General. If you thought I was unfair with you, you should have seen me with them. Mrs. Brashler almost resigned. When I came back from here and told her about my plans to relocate, she was overjoyed."

"So was I," Gin admitted, laughing. "When I saw you in your office that day, I wanted to blurt out my love for you, but it made me so angry that I flew into a blind rage."

"I think we've developed a very bad habit of shouting senselessly at each other." Noah looked down at

her lovingly. "I'm going to have to remember to silence your words with kisses from now on." He
claimed her lips again, letting his linger over hers,
then took a ragged breath. "Ginny," he said hoarsely,
running a hand possessively over the curve of her hip,
"doctors aren't supposed to lose their sensibilities, but
whenever I'm near you I can't even think straight."

"You do a good job of pretending, Noah Grady.
I believed all those things you told me about coming
here because of greed . . . and the child. You sounded
so convincing."

Noah laughed huskily. "Allow me to show you the
purpose of my relocation," he said. His hand reached
up to cup her breast.

Gin clung to him for a long moment, then took a
deep, trembling breath. "So I was right. You came
to Kentucky to seduce me," she said, but her accusation sounded more like an invitation.

"When I came here the first time, I used the baby
as an excuse," Noah said seriously. "Then I discovered I wanted you more than anything in my life. I
came back to try to convince you I loved you, but I
also wanted you to realize how much you needed me.
By not touching you I tried to show you that there
was more between us than physical desire."

"Then you're happy about the baby?" Gin asked.

"Uh-huh," Noah murmured against her earlobe,
pushing her back into the soft pillows of the sofa.
"Very happy. I'm looking forward to fatherhood." He
placed his hands on the lower part of her abdomen.
"Have you felt the baby move yet?"

Gin was touched by his action, and tears rushed
to her eyes. "No, it's too soon," she explained, her
voice thick with emotion. "I'm barely into my third
month."

Noah brushed a tear from her cheek and kissed her

again, a long, lingering caress as his hands roamed to the bare skin of an exposed thigh, tracing light circles on her trembling body.

He pressed his body against hers, his tongue exploring her mouth, then sat up, running a hand across his silver-gray eyes. "I'm thirty years old, Ginny," he said, his voice low and ragged. "Much too mature for groping around on a couch with the woman I love." He took her hand in his. "I know a preacher over beyond Hyden who specializes in clandestine weddings. I think he might even consider a ceremony without a shotgun. Will you go with me?"

"Is this another proposition?" she asked, teasing.

He nodded. "Do you accept this time, or do I have to abduct you? I'm not going to let you out of my sight until you're mine."

"Oh, yes," Gin said. "I accept." She watched him kiss her fingertips, studying him seriously. "Do you want to go back to Minnesota, Noah?" she asked. "We don't have to stay here."

"Right now there's only one place I want to go, and that's to your apartment, but in answer to your question, no. Sandy Point is like chicken. I've developed a fondness for it, and if you agree I think we can help Douglas make Whitney Clinic the best medical center in the Appalachians. Do you concur, junior partner?"

"Only if you don't continue to treat every beautiful woman in the entire state for headaches," she answered, grinning.

"Are you telling me you're going to be a jealous wife as well as a stubborn one?" he teased back.

"Oh, Noah, I can't believe we've let something as foolish as pride interfere in our relationship for all these months."

"Ginny, we have the rest of our lives to make up

for it." He glanced at his watch. "But if you don't stop talking and start moving, I'm going to pick you up bodily and carry you out of here. Now, what will Douglas think of that?"

"I can't imagine," Gin said, "and to tell you the truth, I really don't care."

"Shame on you, Miss Selton." Noah laughed and wrapped her in his arms, kissing her lightly on the lips. "Ginny"—his voice grew husky—"there's this tribe in New Guinea that has a very interesting obsession about pregnancy. They believe that the more frequently a husband makes love to his wife, the stronger their child will be."

"Isn't that a primitive superstition, Noah?" Gin smiled up at him, wrapping her arms around his neck.

"Very primitive," he answered, running his hands over her hips. "And very intriguing."

"Are you suggesting we perpetuate this notion?" Gin asked, trembling.

"I'm a pagan at heart," he said, swooping her up in his arms. "Let's find that preacher. I consider producing a strong child my husbandly obligation." He cocked a dark eyebrow at her. "Unless you have any objections."

Gin rested her head on his shoulder. "No objections," she said softly. "In fact, I can hardly wait."

WATCH FOR
6 NEW TITLES EVERY MONTH!

Second Chance at Love

Second Chance at Love

____ 06195-6 **SHAMROCK SEASON #35** Jennifer Rose
____ 06304-5 **HOLD FAST TIL MORNING #36** Beth Brookes
____ 06282-0 **HEARTLAND #37** Lynn Fairfax
____ 06408-4 **FROM THIS DAY FORWARD #38** Jolene Adams
____ 05968-4 **THE WIDOW OF BATH #39** Anne Devon
____ 06400-9 **CACTUS ROSE #40** Zandra Colt
____ 06401-7 **PRIMITIVE SPLENDOR #41** Katherine Swinford
____ 06424-6 **GARDEN OF SILVERY DELIGHTS #42** Sharon Francis
____ 06521-8 **STRANGE POSSESSION #43** Johanna Phillips
____ 06326-6 **CRESCENDO #44** Melinda Harris
____ 05818-1 **INTRIGUING LADY #45** Daphne Woodward
____ 06547-1 **RUNAWAY LOVE #46** Jasmine Craig
____ 06423-8 **BITTERSWEET REVENGE #47** Kelly Adams
____ 06541-2 **STARBURST #48** Tess Ewing
____ 06540-4 **FROM THE TORRID PAST #49** Ann Cristy
____ 06544-7 **RECKLESS LONGING #50** Daisy Logan
____ 05851-3 **LOVE'S MASQUERADE #51** Lillian Marsh
____ 06148-4 **THE STEELE HEART #52** Jocelyn Day
____ 06422-X **UNTAMED DESIRE #53** Beth Brookes
____ 06651-6 **VENUS RISING #54** Michelle Roland
____ 06595-1 **SWEET VICTORY #55** Jena Hunt
____ 06575-7 **TOO NEAR THE SUN #56** Aimée Duvall

All of the above titles are $1.75 per copy

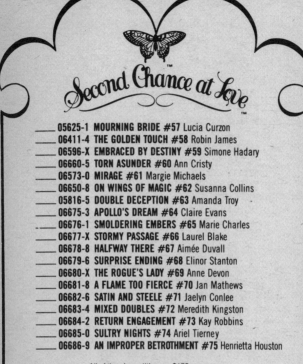

WHAT READERS SAY ABOUT
SECOND CHANCE AT LOVE

"SECOND CHANCE AT LOVE is fantastic."
—*J. L., Greenville, South Carolina**

"SECOND CHANCE AT LOVE has all the romance of the big novels."
—*L. W., Oak Grove, Missouri**

"You deserve a standing ovation!"
—*S. C., Birch Run, Michigan**

"Thank you for putting out this type of story. Love and passion have no time limits. I look forward to more of these good books."
—*E. G., Huntsville, Alabama**

"Thank you for your excellent series of books. Our book stores receive their monthly selections between the second and third week of every month. Please believe me when I say they have a frantic female calling them every day until they get your books in."
—*C. Y., Sacramento, California**

"I have become addicted to the SECOND CHANCE AT LOVE books...You can be very proud of these books....I look forward to them each month."
—*D. A., Floral City, Florida**

"I have enjoyed every one of your SECOND CHANCE AT LOVE books. Reading them is like eating potato chips, once you start you just can't stop."
—*L. S., Kenosha, Wisconsin**

"I consider your SECOND CHANCE AT LOVE books the best on the market."
—*D. S., Redmond, Washington**

*Names and addresses available upon request